CERULEAN

HOLLY THORNE

hollythornebooks.com

CHAPTER 1

Elise took another drag from the cigarette balancing between two frigid fingers, trying her best to ignore the incessant quivering in her bones. The leaves beneath her shoes glittered with frost in the burgeoning sunlight and she stamped on them to warm her feet.

God, it was cold—and she was an idiot. She'd left her coat at the edge of the wood clearing so it wouldn't smell of smoke, but that wasn't doing much good for her now.

She huddled close to the fallen log behind her, drawing her bare legs to her chest. The sun was up, though only just, and everything was grey frost and morning shadow. Elise's heart bolstered. This was the time of day she lived for; it was this pathetic ritual that kept her days afloat.

The cigarette was nearly burnt down to the quick now. Elise curled her other hand against the washed-out black t-shirt, gleaning the meagre body heat from her stomach. It was her sister's, the t-shirt, not that she'd ever notice—she had about fifty of the things. Elise liked this one. It had a fairy printed in grey on it, albeit a scantily clad, outrageously posing one, but Elise had a thing for anything cute that might dwell in the forest.

Elise flicked the cigarette—she was getting good at that now—and the ash fell into her blonde hair, stark against the black of the t-shirt. She swiped the ash off and stood up, stamping the cigarette into the mud, a tiny little grave amongst others that she'd created in the last few weeks of coming out here. Maddy would love that metaphor. Standing up, Elise frowned. She didn't want to be thinking about her sister.

With arms nearly too numb to function, she whipped the t-shirt off, rightening the cream coloured dress she had on underneath and feeling something close to resentment at the sight of it. Without the black t-shirt she was just Elise again—boring Elise, anxious Elise. The familiar heaviness settled around her again as she stuffed the t-shirt into a plastic bag and stuffed that in a crevice beneath the log.

Retrieving her coat, she began the walk back to the house, desperate to return to the warmth of it, but already mourning the girl she left behind in the graveyard of cigarettes.

She pulled the sliding patio doors open and blew out an audible breath at the heat of the kitchen before shrugging off her coat, tossing it over a stool. She glanced at the clock hanging from a beam then over at the bowl on the kitchen table—still untouched—and sighed. Crossing over to the kitchen counter, she picked up a box of cereal and slammed it next to the bowl before jogging up the stairs.

'Maddy!' She swung around the banister and knocked on her sister's door. She pushed it open, surprised it wasn't locked. 'Dude, get up.' The lump on the bed groaned and Elise rolled her eyes, slapping at it. 'It's Monday, Maddy, for god's sake. At least pretend to make an effort until midweek. You've got like twenty minutes before the bus. You can still make it.'

'I'll get the next one,' Maddy murmured, sticking her hands further under her pillow.

'I don't want to get that one. It gets in too late. Besides, you—'

'Oh my god, just get the bus on your own!' The mass of long hair on the pillow moved, twitching like a black octopus with its tentacles splayed. Maddy was always teasing her hair with her broken-toothed comb. Elise didn't know how she could run a brush through the tangled mess most

4

days. 'Don't be such a baby.'

In the ensuing silence, Maddy sighed though it could hardly be heard over the sudden thudding of Elise's heart. 'Fuck you, Maddy,' she finally said.

Elise heard a mumbled *ouch* as she slammed the bedroom door shut. Back downstairs, she pulled on her shoes and coat, biting the inside of her lip against the anger. It wasn't enough to quell the anxiety, it never was, but it took the edge off. She left for the bus a whole twenty minutes early; being the last one to board and fighting for a seat during Monday morning rush hour was literally the worst thing she could imagine.

It was too bloody cold. Elise sighed silently, curling her hand around her bus pass in her pocket, just to check it was there. She had some loose change too, just in case it got declined or whatever. So many just in cases. One day, Elise would love to just roll out of bed and stumble into life like Maddy seemed to do so bloody effortlessly. But then again, Maddy was a bit of a waster, so maybe not.

When the bus finally came, the increase in her heartrate was almost a relief, bringing some life back into her frozen body. She scanned the windows before the bus had even rolled to a stop. There were a couple of free seats. She relaxed slightly.

It was better on the bus. Once it got moving, she leaned her head against the window and put in her earphones, double-checking that they were plugged into her phone properly. A sound leak would be the death of her. She put on some heavier stuff this morning, trying to resurrect even an aura of the girl she'd left in the woods.

She was early to English, her first lesson, just how she liked it. She leant against the wall and slid down to sit on the floor of the corridor, music still trilling through her earphones. There was no one around so she turned it up and closed her eyes slightly, pretending she felt as carefree as she looked.

Maddy never came to English. Big surprise. As other students filed into the room, Elise rattled off a text and chucked her phone next to her textbook. *Idiot.*

She got a reply halfway through the lesson.

Maddy: Fell back to sleep, but on my way now, prommy x

CHAPTER 2

Maddy opened her mouth and executed a yawn, adding in some vocals to make it extra obnoxious. She scrubbed her watery eyes and leaned back in her chair. Her feet were drawn up to her chest, toes on the edge of the table, making the whole thing precarious.

'I'm wiped,' she murmured.

'Same,' the boy beside her replied, ruddy head held in a palm. Maddy glanced at Phil from the corner of her eye. He'd tried eyeliner this morning. He was getting better at it, but the flicks were too long. He tried to make them like hers, despite her telling him he just didn't have the eyes for it.

'Off we go then!' their lecturer said from the front of the class. Maddy roused herself along with the rest of the students, swinging her feet down from the table and picking up her camera.

They were off to take some pictures and despite the fact that she'd be freezing her tits off, Maddy didn't mind. Miles better than being holed up in the classroom.

They paraded down the street to where a weird sculpture-cum-climbing frame was. The rubbery ground was spongey under their feet and Maddy jumped up and down on it a couple of times to thaw out her numb extremities. Their lecturer began removing some balls from a bag—they were taking action shots today.

Maddy grabbed one then dragged Phil and his shitty eyeliner over to the edge of the area where they could doss around in peace.

'So, you gonna tell me about your date or what?' Maddy asked. They were both looking down at the screens of their cameras, altering the settings their lecturer had told them.

'Oh my god,' Phil began, voice conspiratorial, 'so don't be mad but I did something kind of fucked up.'

'Do tell.' Maddy found the right settings and pointed the camera at her classmates who were already throwing their balls around.

She liked hearing about Phil's nights out but since she wasn't eighteen yet, they made her kind of jealous too. Thank god her birthday was soon.

'So, you know Sandy Crack, the drag queen?' he said.

'Don't know her personally, but yeah.'

'Well, I gave her a BJ in the disabled toilets.'

Maddy lowered her camera. 'Isn't he, like, sixty?'

'Yeah, that's why it's so fucked! But I dunno, I was drunk and it wasn't that weird or anything.'

'*Okaaay*,' Maddy drew out. 'So what about this date?'

Phil waved his small, chubby hand. 'He bailed. We're rescheduling for next Saturday instead.'

'Fair.'

'You signed up yet?'

Maddy shook her head. Phil had signed up for whatever gay dating site he was part of before he'd turned eighteen but Maddy wanted to wait. She was kind of excited, nervous too, but would rather die than let Phil know that.

'Birthday's soon. Might as well wait. Besides, you said you'd set me up.'

Phil blew out a breath. 'Yeah, if there was anyone fit around here, which there's not. Believe me, I've been looking.'

Maddy snorted. 'Don't worry about it. Also, don't forget it's the party next Saturday. You can bring that boy but bail on me and I'll kill you.'

'Oh shit. Yeah don't worry, I'll do the date earlier in the day or something. Have you sent off for your provisional

ID yet?'

Maddy grimaced. 'Fuck. Not yet.'

'Get it sorted, idiot. No way are we not going out after the party.'

'I will, I will! Now shut up and go over there so I can take some pics of you throwing that bloody ball.'

CHAPTER 3

Cerulean arrived in the city at night, a sack slung over her shoulder that Risarial had hastily thrown together per her request. She knew her youngest sister had wandered here with nothing but her glamour, but Cerulean loved to make things easier for herself if she could.

The outer roads were like veins—narrow and quiet and threading in the direction of some eventual beating heart. Cerulean could smell life on the winter wind, hear its base deep beneath her feet. She followed the roads until they opened up into a vast, paved area, riddled with life. Her first thought was of an ant's nest, one she'd stamped on to rile up the minibeasts and send them running.

It was a night of revels and Risarial had told her most weeks were bookended with them. It was hard to know which to join—most doorways were teeming with humans, most wearing nothing but shocks of colour wrapped around their torsos and shoes with needle heels. Cerulean's nostrils flared. She'd been to a club once with her sisters but that time was different; she'd been there for Earlie and kept under the watchful gaze of Risarial. Now she was alone. Now she was free.

She took an alleyway that was bleeding with pink neon light. At the end of it, some human girls were bantering with a large blocky man. He had a smile on his wide face but his folded arms warded the girls away from whatever they were insisting.

On the floor at Cerulean's feet sat a man, a small dog curled in his lap. It turned its face up to Cerulean and gave a small bark.

'Shut it, Cassie,' the man snapped back. He said to Cerulean, 'Ah, she won't hurt yer. Just protective, that's all.'

Cerulean eyed the man with his tatty blanket and bearded face. She looked back at the neon club to see that the girls were now gone.

'You don't want to join the revel?' Cerulean asked the man.

'Eh?' He glanced at the club and chuckled. 'Back in my prime, back in my prime. They's friendly in there, thems lot. Always happy to stroke Cassie, aren't they Cassie?' The man lowered his face to the animal, the dog's tongue lapping at his chin like a lizard. It was vile. Cerulean grinned.

'You holing up somewhere?' the man asked, nodding at the bag slung over her shoulder.

'Excuse me?'

'You got a home or you begging?'

'Neither,' she said.

The man nodded. He looked up at her, shielding his eyes against the pink lights. 'Ah shit, I thought you was a man!' He chuckled again. 'Fuck me. Hey sweetheart, sorry to ask, but don't suppose you got any spare change on you? Don't ask for much. Just a coffee in the morning, maybe. Just a hot drink.'

Cerulean shrugged the bag from her shoulder and dropped into a squat beside it. Money was one of the things Risarial had packed for her, a whole wad of it, though she wasn't sure why. She could just as easily conjure the notes and coins herself.

She sat down next to the man, ignoring the low rumble from the dog. From her sack, she pulled out a twenty-pound note.

'Ah, I don't need that much, love.'

Cerulean regarded the note. She didn't have any smaller quantities. 'Would you like to gain it from me?'

'Eh?'

Cerulean folded the note up. It was plasticky, threatening to spring open against her palm. 'Answer me some questions and the money is yours. All is fair.'

After a moment of looking at her groggily, the man shrugged. 'Alright.'

'Which city is this?'

'Manchester, petal.'

Cerulean nodded. She had thought as much. She'd been here before though heavens knows which part of it.

'Do you know where I might find lodgings for the night?'

'I'm assuming you mean a hotel or something, not some piss-stained doorway?'

'Company would be preferable.' Cerulean smiled as two girls trotted by them.

'Eh?'

'It was hard being me, you know.' Cerulean kicked her long legs out, crossing them at the ankle. 'So many damn appearances to uphold. You wouldn't believe the amount of planning that went into visiting the bordello just the once. Absolutely not worth it, my friend. All that fawning.' Cerulean rolled her eyes. 'Heavens, I wish glamour worked on my own kind.'

'Sorry, I ain't following here.' The man turned, his face a mask of confusion. 'You asking me for a hotel or a brothel?' He squinted his eyes at her. 'You're one of those gays, aren't yer? You might want to try down by the canal there. Places for you there, a whole lot of them.'

'By the water?'

'Yeah, right. Follow the rainbow.' The man cackled. 'Can't steer you wrong, place is plastered with them flags.'

Cerulean clapped the man on the shoulder. 'I love a quest.' She slapped the note into his hands and stood up. 'May we meet again.'

CHAPTER 4

'I'm inviting Martha.'

Maddy let her head drop back against the sofa with a groan. She had a can of beer cupped in her hands and sat flicking the tab with a restless finger, much to her sister's annoyance. 'Really?'

'Yep.' Elise nodded, adding her name to the list. She sat crouched between the sofa and coffee table, one hand poised in the air as her hair threatened to tumble into her face as she wrote.

'Urgh, but she's so…*urgh.*'

'Don't be a dick. She's nice.'

'She's a literal robot. And her name's *Martha.*'

'What's wrong with that?'

Maddy took a sip of beer, shaking her head as the coldness hit her teeth. 'No one our generation should be called Martha.'

'Don't worry, you'll be drunk. You're always nice when you're drunk.' Elise capped her pen and hoisted herself onto the sofa. 'I think I'm done. I can't think of anyone else.'

'Good. It's just a party. You don't need to write a list.'

'I'm sending out the invitations tomorrow.'

Maddy lifted her head off the sofa. 'You bloody are not.' Catching Elise's grin, she shook her head. 'Dick.'

'Who are you inviting?' Elise asked.

'Anyone and everyone, since Mum and Dad can't be fucked to be here for their daughters' eighteenth.'

Elise pursed her lips. 'Yeah, that sucks.'

Maddy lifted her beer. 'But hey, at least we get to drink all their booze. In a few days it'll even be legal.'

'Yeah, fuck them,' Elise said quietly.

Maddy raised her eyebrows then slung an arm around Elise's shoulders. 'Don't be sad, you still have me.'

'My evil twin.'

'Shut up. You mean the good looking one.'

'We are literally identical.'

'We bloody are not. Not these days.' Maddy sighed, taking another noisy sip from her can. 'You should have gone down the emo route with me. Could you imagine?'

'Rather not.' She threw Maddy's arm off her. 'Did you send off for your provisional?'

'Oh, fucking fuck it.'

Elise shook her head. 'Maddy.'

'I'll do it now.' Maddy dropped her can onto the table and jumped up. 'I'm doing it now.'

'Way too late. Way, way too late.'

'It won't be!' Maddy shouted from the stairs. 'I'll manifest it!'

CHAPTER 5

Cerulean eyed the expanse of smooth, dark skin before her, blinking drowsily. The long, golden lashes of her eyes were clumped with sleep but she didn't want to move in order to clean them. The back in front of her was definitely human. At the top, on the left shoulder blade, was a tattoo of a star with some script flowing from it. Probably a name, but Cerulean wasn't versed well enough in human to say for sure.

She rolled onto her back and yawned loudly. When the body next to her roused, she turned over and embraced it. '*Shhh,*' she soothed. 'Back to sleep, pretty one.'

The body stilled again and Cerulean chuckled. Judging by the light straining through the curtains, it was getting on in the morning. In a moment, Cerulean would pack up her bag and get on with her day but for now she was content to languish in the comfort of the bed she laid on.

She rolled her head to the side, now facing the sleeper's closed eyes and gently sloping nose. This close, she could see all the pores and impurities of her skin, and the light sheen of oil lying over it all.

So far, everything about this realm both disgusted and fascinated her. It was the seventh night she'd managed to make a home for herself with somebody else. Humans weren't difficult to compel she found, especially the ones she mingled with at revels. Spirits were strong here and it seemed merely a whiff of a tumbler made them putty in

Ceruleans large, strong hands. On the one or two occasions they hadn't been so obliging, Cerulean had sighed in faux resignation and utilised her glamour to soften the deal.

One time, a woman had been keeping a man in the house which would explain her reluctance to bring Cerulean home. It was a major tickle for her to wake up the next day with the woman beside her and the man on the floor, slack in slumber and clothed in nothing but a pair of threadbare sleep shorts. She felt no remorse for taking his place in his bed but prided herself on not taking his girl. It wasn't fun when they didn't want to parlay.

She wondered idly where she'd make her home tonight. She found herself fatigued at the thought of another conquest, another whirl around a noisy, stinky room, hedging her bets on who would be most obliging. Dare she say she was getting bored? Already? Cerulean chuckled to herself. Risarial would roll her eyes at that. She always said Cerulean didn't have the patience for something as tricky as love. Cerulean raised her arms above her head and cracked her knuckles. She always did like proving Risarial wrong.

She knew her oldest sister had claimed another's home for herself but that whole deal seemed like a drag to Cerulean. She wondered instead where Earlie had slept during her time earthside. She didn't think it was with her mortal. Knowing her sister, she probably housed herself beneath bushes and logs, cosying up with the worms and woodlice. Unfortunately, hedonism was Cerulean's middle name. She wasn't exactly the hedge-dwelling type.

With a bracing breath, she rolled up and out of the bed in one motion, moving her blonde, mop-like curls off her forehead as she glanced around for her clothes.

She raised her shirt to her face when she found it. It was musty with dried sweat and the liquids that had been spilled on her the night before. With a wave of a hand, the material, when she wafted it next, smelled only of the rose-scented waters of the lake back home. She smiled wistfully then shoved the thing over her head. Damned if she was going to get homesick yet. She had a bargain to fulfil.

CHAPTER 6

Maddy kicked her heels against the wall of the corner shop, impatiently waiting for Phil's sandy-blonde head to reappear. There was a seagull at the threshold of the shop and Maddy watched it, mentally egging it to enter. As it was getting close, pecking at crumbs just inside the door, a couple of boys in joggers kicked at it as they passed and the bird flew away in a fit of outraged flapping.

Maddy frowned openly as the boys walked by her. Fucking chavs. This side of their town was full of them, the small shopping precinct being the centre point between Maddy's more affluent neighbourhood and the rougher area on the other side.

The boys were probably heading to the park which was an absolute cesspool of their type at night, especially on a Friday. Maddy had always found it fun to hang out there, riling them up, until the time she got punched in the nose by some girl with awful hair extensions. She hadn't ventured to the park after dark since.

When Phil appeared a moment later, she forgot about the chavs and kicked off the wall to meet him.

'Thank *youuuu*,' she sang, happily hearing the clanging of vodka bottles inside the tote bag he held.

'Got you some ciggies, too.'

'Oh, much obliged,' she said, bobbing her head at him.

'You're welcome, my lady. Here. You carry it.' He thrust the bag at her and she slung it over her shoulder. 'So, what time do you want me tomorrow?'

It was early evening, the sky dark as sin already. The two walked towards the pizza shop to pick up theirs and Elise's orders. One of the only good things about their parents being perpetually AWOL was that they could eat whatever the hell they wanted, funded by the loose change Dad left around the house.

Maddy shrugged. 'Whenever. Doesn't start *officially* until eight.'

'Who have you invited?'

'Everyone,' Maddy said with a mischievous grin. 'Don't tell Elise.'

Phil whistled. 'Girl gonna be *piiiissed*.'

'Elise is always pissed. She needs to chill out.'

The girl working behind the counter spotted them and turned to pick up their pizza boxes. God, Maddy had the hots for that girl. Truth be told, she would prefer to order from the chippy next door but seeing that girl smile at her as she handed over their food made her fucking week. Why does short hair make every girl a million times hotter?

'Mum says nope to a fire pit,' Maddy continued as they made their way back outside. 'But I say fuck her. Least I can do to get my own back. Besides, more people outside means less house trashing for her.'

Phil screwed up his face. He had yellow eyeshadow on his lids, drawn in a pointy, triangular way that made Maddy think of drag queens. Probably inspired by the old queen he was sucking off at his visits to the gay bar. The image made Maddy's lips twist.

'They really not going to be there?' he asked.

'Nope. I mean, it's good for the party—they were gonna go to my aunt's anyway for that. But yeah, it sucks. They've apparently got some super important work thing going on. As usual.' Maddy shrugged. 'Anyway, I don't care.'

'Fuck off. Yeah you do.'

'Okay, a bit. Well, it's just shit! They're so emotionally negligent. Like no wonder me and Elise are so fucked up.'

22

Back at the house, they dumped their pizza boxes on the coffee table in the lounge and Maddy blew out an obnoxiously loud raspberry at the sight of Elise sitting on the carpet in a puddle of multicoloured balloons.

'What the fuck, Elise.'

Elise smiled. 'Shut up, I'm about to pass out here.'

'Didn't realise we were turning six.'

'I love balloons,' Phil said, kicking at one with a socked foot. Maddy kicked it back and they went like that for a while until it popped and Elise chastised them.

Plonking herself on the sofa, Maddy pulled her pizza towards herself. 'Fuck, I am *starving*.'

'Same,' Elise sighed, sitting down next to Maddy and flicking the top of the pizza box her sister pointed at. 'You got me veggie, right?'

Maddy rolled her eyes. 'Yes. I also got you your vodka and *orange juice*.' She screwed up her face. 'Who voluntarily chooses *orange juice* as a mixer?'

'Me.' Elise shrugged, biting the tip off a pizza slice. A chunk of green pepper fell onto her white top, staining it red with tomato sauce. Elise wiped at it for a moment before giving up. 'Coke is too fizzy. I can drink more with just juice.'

Maddy grinned. 'Oh, you are so getting wasted.'

'Here's hoping,' Elise replied, eyes a little distant.

'Hey Elise, are you still coming out with me tomorrow?' Phil asked.

Elise nodded, mouth full. She glanced at her sister, swallowed, and said, 'Don't suppose you can get any fake ID before tomorrow?'

'No.' Maddy dropped her head against the back of the sofa. 'I tried but no one looks remotely like me. And yes, I know I'm a massive idiot.'

In reality, she was absolutely pissed at herself for leaving it too late, not an unfamiliar feeling at all, but she did have a small teary moment when the post arrived earlier without her provisional.

'Yes, you are,' Elise agreed.

'You can always try your passport,' Phil said, mollifyingly. 'I know it's out of date but some places won't care. I bet Rainbows doesn't.'

Rainbows was their local gay bar. The plan had been to start there before getting a taxi into Manchester and trying out the bigger clubs along Canal Street.

Nodding, Maddy said, 'I'll give it a shot, for sure.'

'Get you some fanny.'

'Oh fuck, Phil, that is so gross.'

Elise laughed. 'Never say that word again, Phil.'

'Fannies are disgusting,' Phil agreed with a grin, unrepentant. 'You're right.'

'They are not,' Maddy said.

'They are. I'm allergic.'

'You also seem to be allergic to dick your own age. Elise, did you know Phil is getting it on with some dude old enough to be his granddad?'

'Gross,' said Elise.

Phil wrinkled his nose. 'Yeah, I was gonna tell you but I went out with him night before last, you know, just as ourselves. And I dunno, it was kind of weird. Without all his makeup and shit, he was just kinda…'

'A dirty old man?' supplied Maddy.

'Yeah. I'm not going there anymore. The boy I'm seeing tomorrow is only twenty.'

Maddy snorted. 'An improvement.' She turned to her sister. 'How was your therapy sesh earlier?'

'It was fine,' Elise said lightly. 'Had some good parent-fodder this time.'

Maddy snorted again. 'Don't you always?'

'What's your therapist like?' Phil asked. 'She fit?'

Elise tilted her head side to side. 'Kinda, if you like older women.'

'I do,' Maddy said.

Elise ignored her. 'She's pretty cool. Down to earth. Not too professional.'

'When d'you think you'll be fixed?' Maddy asked.

'Never if it means Mum has to stop paying.'

Maddy smiled. 'You're more of a shit than I am sometimes. I'm proud.'

'Well, same cloth and all that.' Elise shook her head. 'Anyway. Enough parent talk. They suck. Whatever. It's our birthday tomorrow.'

Maddy nodded, more than happy to agree.

On the other side of Elise, Phil sighed dramatically. 'Finally. Been waiting years for you to catch up with me.'

'Oh, shut up,' Maddy told him. 'You're literally two months older than us.'

'The distance is vast. I have way more sexual experience than you now.'

'I don't want your sexual experiences.'

Phil turned to Elise. 'Have you popped your cherry yet?'

Elise shook her head but it was Maddy who answered. 'Has she hell. I want to get her laid tomorrow. Elise has already agreed.'

'I have not.'

'What's your type?' Phil asked. 'I'll help.'

Elise hesitated. 'I dunno. Blonde, I guess.'

'I'm assuming we're talking guys?' he asked, and Elise nodded. 'Alright.' Phil stretched out his arms and pretended to crack his knuckles. 'I'll wingman you.' He nodded to Maddy. 'You too.'

'Don't need your help, but thanks,' Maddy said.

'Please, you've been asking for my help for months, oh lesbian of desperation.'

Maddy frowned. 'I'm not desperate.' Her face cleared and she grinned. 'Just horny.'

'Urgh, Maddy,' Elise complained. 'Don't be gross.'

Maddy nudged her. 'You're gross. At least I've done it.'

'Yeah, not with a girl though,' Phil said. 'We're getting you online first thing tomorrow.'

Maddy nodded. 'Fine.'

CHAPTER 7

Cerulean stood on a bridge, watching the shop across the road. It was early morning and the air was different to yesterday. Cerulean was amused. The first time she'd stood there, she'd been baffled at the humans running around in their cars, smogging the air up with their fumes. They were so focused, so furious. Cerulean didn't understand. But today, her second week earthside, she was starting to get used to how different days tasted and the patterns the humans would repeat.

Her favourite pattern was the one taking place at the shop she watched. It was busy, full of scurrying humans scrabbling for the hot drinks people behind the counter would gift them. Cerulean watched the ritual a couple more times before deciding to join in.

It was fun, pretending. Cerulean joined the queue, squatting down to eye up the food stuffs behind the glass. When it was her turn, Cerulean pointed at a drink on the menu and down at a sandwich.

'Name, please?'

When Cerulean gave it, the girl gave her a second glance but said nothing.

'Collect you order at the end, thank you.'

Bowing slightly, Cerulean joined the huddle of humans waiting for their drinks, smiling at each of them in turn. Barely a one smiled back. Next to them was a wooden countertop full of little packets. Cerulean tilted her head.

Sugar one of them read. Cerulean snagged five.

Once she received her order, Cerulean took it back to her spot on the bridge, leaning back against it and crossing her legs. She was smiling as she took the lid off her drink, inhaling the florally, herbaceous scent of it. They were kind of adorable, these angry little humans. She supposed if she lived for as short a time as they did, she'd hurry all over the place too.

She took a sip. It wasn't like the floral teas of home—of rose and chamomile and lavender—but with the added sugar sachets, it was better.

As she fumbled with the wrapper of her sandwich, a group of girls caught her eyes. They were all dressed the same, in baggy denim and padded coats, and each held a steaming cup in their hands. Cerulean glanced down at her own loose shirt and even looser trousers, wondering if she should be feigning cold.

Looking back up, she caught a couple of the girls smiling at her. She raised her drink and smiled back and they turned away. Cerulean grinned. So damn easy it was almost boring.

And yet—her grin turned wry—she was no closer to snaring her mortal. Cerulean angled her head to the sky. There was barely a blot of white up there. It tended to start out that way, she found, before clouds descended around late morning. She supposed she was at a bit of a disadvantage, thinking upon it. Risarial had already fore-picked her mortal and Earlie—well—she wasn't as discerning as Cerulean.

She knew Risarial would laugh at that—*you sister— discerning?!*—but love was different. Apparently. In total honesty, so far no one had interested her beyond a single shared night. But heavens, was the hunt *fun*.

CHAPTER 8

Maddy woke to a soft pounding at her door. She rolled over just as Phil entered, carrying two steaming mugs.

'Happy birthday, queen,' he said, handing one of the mugs of tea to Maddy.

Maddy heaved herself up against the headboard, yawning without bothering to cover her mouth. 'Thanks, my dude.'

With her other hand, she reached for her phone. Her parents had messaged—big wow—and she saw Elise had read it but not replied.

'Is it blowing up?'

Maddy snorted. 'Hardly.' She chucked her phone onto the bed. 'What time do you have to be out?'

'Not yet. Not seeing him until 1. Kind of can't be arsed, though.'

'Well, if you bailed you couldn't stay here. I'm taking Elise out for lunch.' Maddy took a sip from her mug. 'I know Mum and Dad not being here is bothering her more than me.'

'Liar.'

Maddy shook her head. 'I just get mad. Elise gets sad. I think that's worse.'

'Fair. Where you off?'

'That hipster place just outside of town. Think she's got it in her head to go vegan so I said I'd treat her to some tofu or some shit.'

'Gonna need more than that to line her stomach before tonight. Fuck, I can't wait,' said Phil.

Maddy nodded her head. 'Same. God, I am so in the mood to get wasted.'

'So. How's it feel to be eighteen?'

'Great. Amazing. Fucking fabulous.'

Phil snorted. 'Here, give me your phone. I wanna set up your thingy.'

Maddy tossed her phone into Phil's lap. Then she leaned her head back and closed her eyes, running her thumbs up and down the heat of her mug as Phil set up her dating profile. 'Don't make me sound like a dick,' she murmured.

'Hey, I'm a pro at this now. I know the drill.' He was silent for a moment before asking, 'You got any nudes on your camera roll?'

'No, go at it.'

She idly watched Phil pick from her numerous selfies, not really giving two shits about which ones he chose. They all looked the same anyway, all kind of moody and pouty, with heavily outlined eyes stark against a pale face.

'Those'll do. You don't want too many or people will think you're a poser.'

'But I am,' Maddy said, offering up a close-eyed, sleepy smirk.

Phil sighed. 'Well, they don't need to know that. What shall I put in your bio?'

'Dunno. Keep it short. Maybe something like, *Maddy from Manchester, seeking boobs. But nothing too big because, ew.*'

'You are so hopeless.' He handed her the phone. 'Do it yourself.'

'Dude, you've set my age bracket way too old. Ew. I'm not *you.*'

Hastily, she narrowed the age range then spent a few minutes bullet-pointing some things about herself as her tea cooled. Nothing too deep, just that she was into photography and looking for something chill, maybe.

'There,' she said finally. 'That'll do.'

'Cool. Keep checking it today. You might find someone to invite round later.'

CHAPTER 9

On her knees by her mirror, surrounded by makeup and discarded outfits, Elise looked into eyes that were already a little glassy and gave a breathy giggle. She was keyed up—obviously. There were just too many variables for the night. She worried about the house getting trashed, about just how many people her stupid sister had invited and about what was going to happen after the party, when they pooled into the city. She'd snuck into the kitchen half an hour ago, tiptoeing past her sister's bedroom door as she blasted her god-awful emo music, and sequestered a bottle of vodka back to her room.

Already almost a quarter of it was gone. Oh well. Elise pulled down her lower eyelid and shakily dragged on some eyeliner. It was doing its damn job.

She was ready before Maddy, a good twenty minutes before people would turn up. *If* they turned up at eight. Maddy said her lot would probably get there later, no doubt already smashed and ready to trash the place.

Elise shook her head and stood up. *Shut up*, she told it.

She ran her eyes over her outfit again. She looked alright—dressed in a thin navy slip and even sheerer tights. It wasn't very Elise but then she wasn't feeling very Elise tonight.

She left her room, surprised to see Maddy's door open, still blaring music, but no Maddy.

She found her twin sitting at the kitchen table, an open

can of cider beside her, tapping at her phone. That damn dating website. She'd been on it all bloody day.

'You look like a hooker,' Maddy said when she spotted her. Elise could see the approval in her eyes and struggled not to smile back.

'And you look like some gothy orphan kid about to top herself.'

Maddy barked out a laugh and turned back to her phone. 'Not far from the truth.'

Elise picked up her boots standing beside the patio door and pulled them on. 'Where's Phil?'

'Dunno, can't get hold of him. If he's ditched me for that boy, I will actually kill him.'

Retrieving her bottle of vodka, Elise unlocked the patio door. 'Keep an ear out for the doorbell, will you?'

'Why, where you going?'

'Back soon.' She slid the door closed behind her and stepped into the night, teeth chattering immediately.

When she got to the bottom of the garden, she turned back. Maddy was still sat at the table, head pillowed in her arms, frowning into the garden, but Elise knew she couldn't see her; she was lost to the shadows now.

She unlocked the gate, stepped into the alley and crossed over into the woods. She'd never visited the woods in the dark, at least not *night-time* dark. Pre-dawn dark was different, it was friendlier, less heavy. This dark freaked her out a little.

Using her phone's torch, she found her spot and sat down on the log. She swayed as she closed her eyes. *Shit.* She let out a snort. Okay, she was going to slow down on the vodka. She took another sip. In a bit.

She leant her elbows on her knees and took a breath, flicking her thumb nail on the mouth of the bottle and making it plink. She hadn't meant to drink so much so fast, that was why she'd taken just the vodka to her room, and no mixer. Just a couple of sips to take the edge off. But after a couple, it hadn't tasted so bad.

Elise opened her eyes again. She didn't know why she was out here, freezing her ass off *again,* only that she was desperate for some relief from her stupid, idiot, dumb brain. She was so, *so* tired of feeling scared all the time. She was an adult now, for god's sake, like an actual one, yet she still felt like some freaked out little kid.

Her therapist had said it was some messed up responsibility thing—because Maddy hadn't heard of the word *responsible* and because her parents were away for work all the time, so Elise had felt a begrudging pressure to step up and be the adult for her and Maddy. That having started at a young age had been too much and *voila,* her anxiety monster spawned.

When she felt herself getting teary, Elise roused herself to go back to the house. Okay, so coming out here hadn't helped. Shit. She forgot vodka messed her up sometimes.

Just as she reached the alleyway, her phone pinged.

Maddy: Your robot friend is here. Pls come back, this is awkward as FUCK

CHAPTER 10

Maddy was lounging in the corner of the sofa, annoyed none of the people she'd invited had turned up yet, when Phil walked in.

'There you are, you utter bastard.' Maddy grabbed his arm and steered him in the direction of the kitchen.

'Sorry,' Phil said, not sounding very sorry at all, as he helped himself from the pile of assorted liquids on the table. He had glittery black eyeshadow on and he looked *good*. 'Date went on a bit.'

'I'm your best friend, dick. Your first love.'

'Yes, you are.' Phil kissed her cheek. He reeked of alcohol already. 'Your place looks cool,' he said.

Maddy nodded. She thought it did too. The kitchen was normal, just somewhere to dump the drinks, but the lounge was lit only by some LED thing they'd bought for cheap online and Maddy had set up her speaker to blast music. Her and Elise fought over what was playing every so often but Maddy didn't really care as long as it was loud. Thank god they lived in a detached house.

'College lot said they'll get here around ten. They're coming from the pub. Elise's friends are alright. I thought they'd all be a bunch of nerds but—' She shrugged.

'Anyone you'd get with?'

Maddy snorted. 'No, they're all straight as *fuck*.'

'Yuck.'

Phil grabbed a plate of crisps that Elise had set out and

retook Maddy's place on the sofa. Maddy plonked herself down next to him, pulling her knees back to her chest and cradling her third—fourth?—can of cider.

'So, how was your date?'

Phil nodded. 'Alright actually. He's nice. Sweet.'

'Didn't think you were into sweet.'

'I'm not really, but he has such a nice face.' He shoved a handful of crisps into his mouth. 'How was your day?'

'Not bad. Lunch was nice. Then I was just killing time until tonight.'

'Any luck on the dating site?'

'Nah. Got a few matches but not really bothered about them. Literally everyone from college is on there though.'

Phil grinned. 'I know. It's mad.'

When Maddy's friends finally arrived, she felt herself perk up and immediately insisted they play a drinking game. Elise sent her a look which definitely said *great, thanks, now everyone's going to know I'm a virgin* but Maddy ignored it and started with the first *never-have-I-ever* question.

It was her fave. She always impressed herself with the level of grossness she could conjure up for the questions and took pride in the amount of times she drank compared to others, which she knew wasn't the point but whatever.

She'd finished her can by the end of the game and was more than ready to start a round of *Ring of Fire*. She saw Elise eye up the empty cup dubiously and prayed her sister would be the one to drink the forfeit at the end. She would literally pay to see that.

But, alas, it was Phil who lost and he chugged the dirty pint like a champ to the chants of *chug, chug, chug*. Maddy slapped him on the back afterwards, grinning at the look on his face. There was milk in that pint somewhere, as well as juice; Maddy could never.

She leaned over. 'Be sick and I'll kill ya.'

When she next suggested clearing the kitchen table for a game of beer pong, Elise finally snapped, 'Oh my god, Maddy, we don't have to be playing games the whole night.

We can just chill, you know. Like you said, we're not *six*.'

'Fine. Boring.' Maddy retook her spot on the sofa, glowering but not really feeling it. She was on the vodka too now, idly playing with the steel straw with her tongue, feeling the tiny bubbles of the just-poured coke hitting the skin of her face.

A girl from her photography class was smiling conspiratorially at her from the carpet and Maddy smiled back, wondering if she was drunk enough to go there. She knew the girl was gay but was absolutely not her type—at least not when sober. But she'd be depressed as hell if she didn't kiss at least one person on the night of her eighteenth. She'd probably snog Phil at some point, that was a given, but it would be nice to get a kiss from someone she was actually attracted to. She glanced away, telling herself she'd revisit the possibility when she was drunker.

Around eleven, Maddy decided she was finally drunk enough to start the fire pit—if not drunk enough to be kissing her course mates. She expected Elise to go off at her but she only shrugged, eyes all shiny and far away. Maddy grinned; her sister was wasted.

It was freezing outside, no one was going to want to sit out there, but Maddy had it in her head now so she had to follow through.

'I'm probably really fucking flammable right now,' she said, fumbling with the button on her lighter. Her fingers just couldn't get a grip and she snorted at how inept she was.

'Me too,' said Phil, 'but if we go down, we go down together.'

He helped her get the thing lit and they watched the flames for a few drunken, peaceful moments.

'Beautiful,' Maddy said. 'Kinda want to jump in.'

'We have to remember to bank it before we go out.'

'Yeah, yeah. Hey, come with me a sec.'

Maddy darted out a hand and grabbed Phil by his sleeve, dragging him across the garden in earnest.

'Where we going?' he asked.

'I dunno.' She let him go when they reached the gate. 'Elise keeps sneaking out here, in the mornings. She thinks I don't know but my room overlooks the garden for god's sake. I swear, that girl thinks I'm a total dunce.'

'You are.'

'Yeah, but I *notice* things. I notice everything.' At the edge of the wood, where the lights from the house fell away, Maddy turned on her phone torch and gestured at Phil to do the same.

'Mate, we are not going into the woods.'

'Yeah, we are.'

'We're gonna die.'

'I think she's stashing weed.'

'Elise smoking *weed?*' His voice was the most disbelieving that Maddy had ever heard it.

'Hey, my sister might still be a virgin but she's no stiff. I read some of the fan fiction she reads—filthy. She's actually lowkey kind of cray-cray.'

'I believe it, being your twin.'

Okay, so it was kind of weird walking around the woods at night. Maddy shivered, though she wasn't really feeling the cold at this point. She was following some shallowly-trodden path, stepping over exposed roots and brambles.

Behind her, Phil whined. 'Don't like this.'

'Stop being a wimp.'

A few more steps led them to a clearing which was mostly hard-packed dirt. Maddy arced her phone over the area, spotting the trodden butts of numerous cigarettes.

'Elise, you little rebel.'

At her feet was a fallen log. She squatted down, pulling out the plastic bag wedged beneath it. Inside was a black hunk of material and a box of cigarettes.

She up held the material and shook it out. 'Um, what the fuck?'

'That yours?'

'Yeah.' She shoved the t-shirt back in the bag and buried it again. 'Okay, whatever. Cool.'

'Can we go back now? It's bloody freezing.'

At Maddy's shrug, they retraced their steps back to the garden. The firepit was blazing merrily and Phil ascended on it, hands out ready to glean the heat.

When Maddy joined him, her eyes caught someone lounging in one of the lawn chairs, legs stretched out and crossed at the ankles. Maddy didn't recognise her. Over the light of the fire, she looked at her face, at her half-slit eyes and mop of curly blonde hair.

'Oh shit,' she laughed, 'my fire's summoned a lesbian.' Leaving the pit, Maddy flung herself down on the next lawn chair. 'Hi,' she said. 'You're not one of Elise's friends. Do you go to college? Or uni?'

Head lolling against the back of the chair, the girl smiled. 'I do not.'

'So who are you with?'

'Not a one.' The girl grinned boyishly. 'I find myself quite alone and yearning for company.'

Maddy looked back at the gate. 'Dude, did you break in?'

The girl tilted her head. 'It was left open. Did I?'

Maddy laughed. '*Duuuuude.*'

'I heard music.'

Maddy glanced into the kitchen. 'Yeah, we should probs turn it down.' She glanced up at Phil who was doing some weird dance with his eyebrows at her. 'Okay, so I'm super drunk so I don't care that you crashed the party. It's my birthday, by the way. Anyway, wanna come in and get a drink before we get frostbite? Just don't steal anything please.'

The girl unfolded herself from the chair and Maddy was surprised at how tall she was, like a whole head above Maddy.

The kitchen was full of people, like *full,* and as she glanced through to the living room, she saw it was too. She looked around for Elise, expecting to see her shooting stressed looks her way but couldn't spot her anywhere. Probably in her room having a panic attack or something.

41

She gestured to the table with its dwindling alcohol supply and said to the girl, 'Help yourself.' As she watched her choose, she asked, 'What's your name?'

'Cerulean.'

'What?'

The girl leaned in and Maddy felt herself freeze up. '*Ce-ru-le-an.*'

'Oh. Like the colour?' The girl nodded once, blonde curls falling into her slightly smiling eyes. 'That's a cool name. Suits your eyes.'

Suddenly, Phil's hot breath was at her ear. 'I'll just piss off then, shall I? She's probably a serial killer so give me a shout if she tries anything.'

Phil sauntered away and Maddy couldn't help but grin. 'You're not a serial killer, are you?'

Cerulean shook her head once, one hip cocking to lean against the edge of the table. Wow, okay, she was *so* Maddy's type. 'Not to your kind.'

'Sweet.' She looked at the doorway to the lounge. 'Come on. Let's go chill somewhere.'

As they walked, Maddy realised she was the kind of drunk now where every step had to be calculated, the kind of drunk where she was so *aware* of everything despite everything being a little blurry around the edges. She was also a shamefaced horny drunk. Vodka did that to her but wine did it worse; Maddy was glad she hadn't opted for a bottle from her mum's collection of reds.

She found a spot on the floor and pulled Cerulean down with her. The girl stretched her long legs out and Maddy eyed them. The material covering them was some kind of loose linen and they were tucked into weird, pointy boots. She looked more dressed for a ramble in some eighteenth century woodland than a house party, but lesbians dressed pretty weirdly sometimes. God, Maddy only hoped she was gay.

'Is this your home?' Cerulean asked.

'Yep. Well, not mine. My parents'. But they're away.'

Cerulean looked at her. 'And this is your name day revel?'

'Right.' Maddy nodded slowly. 'Eighteen today. My sister too, but she's—' Maddy flicked out a hand, dismissing the sentence. She didn't want to think about Elise right now. 'Well, whatever. We're probably gonna go out in a bit if you want to join us.'

'Go out to where?'

'To a bar.' Maddy eyed her. 'A gay one.'

'I'd be happy to accompany you.' She didn't look at Maddy as she said this. Her eyes grazed over the room again and there was still that little smile on her face. She had such a cheeky face. Maddy was obsessed. 'There is such life in this room. Everything feels…young.'

Maddy looked too, trying to see what she was getting at. 'Some are probably still seventeen. We probably won't all go to the bar.'

Cerulean's eyes were high on the mantelpiece now, scanning the various photos stacked across there. 'Your family?' she asked.

'Yeah,' Maddy sighed. 'That's them.'

'You're not in a lot of them.'

'Good spot. It's because I'm the black sheep of the family who no one wants.' When Cerulean looked at her, Maddy grinned. 'Joking. It's because I took some of the pictures. I do photography at college.' Maddy glanced at the family photos. 'I've got better ones than those. I can show you some, if you want.'

'I would enjoy that.'

'You haven't seen them yet.' Maddy jumped to her feet, palming the wall to steady herself. 'Camera's in my room.'

It was a cheap excuse to get Cerulean alone in her room with her, Maddy knew, but she was too far gone to feel any shame. There were a few people idling in the hallway outside the bathroom and Maddy pushed through them, annoyed at them being there. She'd kick off if someone was in her room but thankfully, it was empty.

She turned on the light, fished her camera out of its bag and sat down on the carpet, back against the bed. Slowly, Cerulean lowered herself beside her. Maddy flicked on the camera and stabbed at the button which would bring up her photos but it was doing that thing again where it jammed up and she had to press it a million times before it obliged.

'Come on,' she muttered, hitting the side of the camera with her open palm. 'God, I need a new one.'

As she fiddled, Cerulean got up again. Maddy watched her walk over to her bookshelf. There weren't many books on there, mainly just random nick-nacks. Cerulean picked up her howlite crystal and rubbed her thumb over it. It was one Elise had given her, to tame the nightmares she had sometimes. She was supposed to keep it under her pillow but she knew she'd lose the damn thing if she did.

'So dull,' Cerulean said, returning the stone to its place with a thud.

'Dull?'

Cerulean plopped down beside her again, her arm brushing Maddy's, warming her all over.

'Dull. Lifeless.' She pulled one knee to her chest, resting her wrist on it. 'Energies are supposed to converge, not diverge. No wonder humankind lead such short lives. This place sucks everything dry.'

Maddy looked up from her camera. 'Are you, like, a scientist or something? A depressed one?'

Cerulean snorted. 'Don't insult me.' She grasped her chin between a thumb and finger and grinned. 'I don't have the beard.'

Lowering her camera to her lap, Maddy reached out and replaced Cerulean's fingers with hers. 'I dunno, I could imagine it,' she said, fingertips tingling. 'Are you single?'

Cerulean's eyebrows twitched. 'Quite.'

'Good.' Maddy dropped her hand. 'That's good.' She tapped a restless finger against the photo on her camera screen—some building silhouetted against an orange, dusky sky. 'You're super attractive.' She snorted. 'No way I'd be saying that if I wasn't a few drinks down, but, whatever, it's true.'

Cerulean's eye turned focused, speculative, and Maddy felt a surge of something close to triumph. 'Attractive for a gatecrasher?'

'Kinda makes you more attractive to be honest. Love a good rebel.'

Cerulean grinned. 'That's me. Just ask my sisters.'

Maddy smiled down at her camera screen, where the face of her own sister looked back at her. She flicked it to the next photo quickly. 'Here,' she said, thrusting the camera at Cerulean. 'Have a look. They're probably shit but it's my thing, so.'

As Cerulean flicked through the photos, Maddy took advantage of their proximity, shuffling closer under the guise of looking at them too. She could mostly just taste and smell alcohol at this point, but there was also another scent coming from the girl beside her. Something herbaceous and earthy. Kind of like lavender but not. More like clary sage. Elise diffused that a lot, to supposedly lessen her anxiety; something her therapist had recommended. Maddy always complained it smelled like piss but wafting from Cerulean it almost made her sway. It made her think of forests at nighttime and the smell of moss when it's wet.

Maddy straightened up, pulling a bracing breath through her nose. God, she was going to fall asleep.

'Let's go back down,' she said, pulling herself up on unsteady legs.

Cerulean rose with her, placing the camera gently on her bed. 'The captures are good,' she said. 'Is that how you see the world?'

'Like what?'

'A lot were shot in dark places. Lots of straight lines and angles. Metal. The sun at day's end, but more of the moon.' Cerulean ran her eyes over Maddy's face. 'I think art is always a reflection of the artist.'

Maddy gave her a pleased smile. 'You know your stuff.

That's hot. And I dunno, I just shoot what I think looks good.' She shrugged. 'Nothing deep.'

As she pulled open her bedroom door, the one opposite opened too, revealing Elise looking a little worse for wear.

'You good?' she asked.

'I was feeling a bit sick,' Elise replied.

Maddy grinned. 'Did you have to do a tactical?'

Elise frowned, shaking her head. 'I feel fine now.' She looked up at Cerulean, then over at Maddy but before Maddy could introduce them, Cerulean had stepped forward and two-handedly cupped Elise by the face. Elise blinked up at her, wide-eyed.

'How uncanny.' She dropped Elise's face then did the same to Maddy.

'Shit, you never seen identical twins before?' Maddy murmured. Despite her dyed black hair, and Elise's blonde, she knew they looked more similar than usual today. Both with black-rimmed eyes and dark clothes, but this was still a whole new level of weird.

'I didn't realise humans could split souls like that. You're both so complete. Almost like two. Heavens, that's fascinating.' She looked between the two of them. 'Look at that.' She let out a breathy laugh. 'Risarial will be simply *green* with envy.'

Elise looked at Maddy and raised her eyebrows. Elise said, 'So, we're going out soon. That okay?'

'Yep.' She put a hand on Cerulean's back and pushed. 'Go on, you absolute weirdo.'

But Cerulean resisted. She looked back to Elise and gestured her ahead first. Elise gave a little smile and complied.

CHAPTER 11

Turned out Rainbows shut at one, which gave Maddy exactly forty-five minutes to enjoy herself, which frankly sucked. At least they let her in with her passport, Phil kept on reminding her, even if it was years out of date and sporting a photo of her where she looked about ten.

They didn't bother with securing seats. They got their drinks and headed straight for the tiny dance floor which, at this point in the night, was packed with writhing queers.

At Phil's insistence, Maddy had ordered a sambuca and lemonade which was new but didn't taste half bad and reminded her of the Black Jack sweets Mum used to give her and Elise as a kid.

She was squished in between Phil and one of Elise's friends. Cerulean was dead in front of her, her thick shoulders tucked in against the two bodies pressed against her, one of them being Elise. Maddy would smile whenever their eyes caught and sometimes take her hand when it brushed in close to her, which was kind of all the time with the dance floor being this packed. One time she did this, Cerulean winked at her and Maddy just about died.

So, it was majorly shit when ten minutes later (because no way was that forty-five), the music stopped and the lights came on and everyone booed—Maddy the loudest—and began filing outside. There were hosts of taxis on the road already, ready to whisk them off to the city.

One of Maddy's college mates hailed one and then

turned to her with a pitying, pouting look that Maddy could have punched her for.

'Sucks you can't come,' she said.

Maddy nodded. She turned to Elise who had been sporting a dazed, don't-know-what-I'm-doing-anymore look for the past hour, and said, 'You coming back with me then?'

Elise frowned. 'No.'

'What? Dude, you're literally swaying.'

'I'm fine. I'm going out.'

'But—' Maddy stopped. In what world was she living in where she had to be sent home and her terrified-of-everything sister was going out clubbing?

'I'll come back with you, Mads,' Phil said.

It was honourable but Maddy shook her head. 'Don't worry about it.'

'Nah. It's your birthday. We'll just have a little afterparty or something.'

Maddy looked at Elise. 'You sure you're okay to go out?'

'*Yes,* Maddy. I want to.' With that, she opened the back door to the taxi and slipped inside.

'Hey.' A hot hand landed on her arm and Maddy looked up into Cerulean's insanely blue eyes. 'I will take care of her. I have sisters too. Both of them ridiculous.'

Maddy bit her lip. In an ideal world, she would have invited Cerulean back to the house with her and Phil. But the world was never ideal was it, so she gave a little smile and said, 'Alright. Cheers. Can I get your number first? You know, so you can tell me if Elise needs rescuing.'

From her back pocket, Cerulean pulled out a phone and handed it to Maddy who hastily punched in her number. She quickly rang it, to be sure she had Cerulean's too.

'Thanks,' she said.

With another wink, Cerulean squeezed into the taxi beside Elise and it sped off.

When the car was out of sight, Maddy dropped her head back and let out a groan.

'Come on,' Phil said, slinging an arm around her shoulders. 'Let's not get all depressy. We'll go out next week, okay?'

With a sigh, Maddy nodded. 'Yep. Sounds good.'

CHAPTER 12

Elise rubbed her eyes, then remembered she was wearing makeup and lowered her hands again, wiping off the greyish eyeliner that had smeared. She had never been this drunk before, not ever. Nothing even felt real anymore. Was she really in a car driving to god knows where, squashed between one of Maddy's friends and another random girl?

Even as the taxi sped down the motorway crazily fast, she didn't feel nervous, which was amazing. Everything was a blur of white and red lights, her eyes too hazy to focus on anything. Perhaps even more miraculously, she hadn't thrown up once.

A shoulder nudged her and she turned her face to the weird girl.

'I have been chartered by your sister to look after you,' she said.

Elise snorted. 'Don't worry about it. I can look after myself.'

'So I thought.' The girl eyed her for a moment. 'Which one of you was born first?'

'Maddy was.'

The girl nodded. 'Oldest sisters are always the most commanding.'

'Yup,' Elise said, though in reality she knew she was the one who had major issues with control.

'I'm not sure I've even caught your name.'

They were in the city now. Elise craned her head around the girl to get a closer look. 'It's Elise,' she said. And then, as an afterthought, 'You?'

The girl grinned again and Elise, this time, was a little caught in it. 'Cerulean. As in the colour.'

'I know what Cerulean means.'

Cerulean grinned wider.

The taxi dropped them off near Canal Street and Elise stood stamping her feet on the pavement while the others decided where to go. She wasn't sure of the name of the club they chose, even when the bouncer whacked a wristband on her. She only knew it was gay and wished her sister was with her.

At the bar, Cerulean offered to buy her a drink. 'Since it is your name day.'

Elise nodded her assent and gave what she hoped was simply a grateful smile. The girl was obviously gay, even if she was stereotyping, and she didn't want to give her the wrong impression. Although to be honest, nothing felt wrong right now. The sea of people on one of the two dance floors was almost comforting, especially after the cold of waiting outside.

'You enjoying yourself?' one of Maddy's friends shouted into her ear. Elise nodded. 'You look so much like Maddy!'

Elise didn't think she had to explain the twin thing so she only nodded again and gave a thumbs up. 'Are you a lesbian too?' the girl went on.

Elise hesitated. She wasn't, but…well, kissing anything didn't seem like a bad idea right now. Probably just the vodka talking, but still. She shook her head slowly.

'Shame,' the girl said.

Elise wanted to laugh. Did a girl just hit on her? She couldn't even remember when a *boy* last did that.

She looked away, suddenly shy. There were so many bodies pressed around her, hot flesh gliding along hers, hair tickling the bare tops of her arms. Elise tried to make her body move like theirs but she'd always been tight, stiff. It was something Maddy heckled her over, something she secretly loathed herself for. She often had solo dance parties in front of her bedroom mirror, all the lights off, only the streetlamps outside her window to gild her, as she tried to make her body do the things that Maddy's could when she danced.

Tonight, she felt almost there.

She took her time with her drink, sipping lightly as she swayed. Having one curled to her chest was strangely soothing. She closed her eyes, letting the music sear her ears.

'Are you still with me?'

She opened her eyes slowly. 'Huh?'

Cerulean leaned towards her. Elise wasn't sure when she'd got so close. 'You look phased out.'

Did she? Elise tried putting on a smile and dancing a bit harder but she honestly couldn't be bothered. She was about one drink away from curling up into a ball on the floor and falling asleep.

She leaned up and said into Cerulean's ear, 'I'm going to the loo.'

She didn't even need it but something made her want to break away from the group and wander somewhere. She found the toilets eventually, her journey made difficult by the unbroken mass of bodies.

It was a unisex toilet and Elise found that a little weird and gross. Guys couldn't aim for anything at the most sober of times.

She abandoned her drink on a ledge on the wall. As the line nudged her to the front, she noticed the two girls in front of her passing back looks and giggling. She leaned her head against the wall and watched them as if from afar.

'You are so cute!' one of them said, mouth touching the rim of her ear.

When a cubicle opened, one of them grabbed her hand and pulled her in with them. They immediately set a handbag on the back of the toilet and pulled out tiny baggies of white powder.

Elise watched on, leaning back against the closed door.

'Hey, do you mind if I…?' She gestured at the toilet.

The girls shook their heads and moved out of her way and Elise peed with the two of them standing in front of her, wiping their nostrils.

Afterwards, one of the girls kissed her on the cheek and they disappeared. The way out of the toilet seemed impossibly long, like a maze which had no turns, just an endless parade of tile. Tile which seemed to be flashing at her. God, her eyes were blurry all of a sudden. She could hardly see.

Elise swallowed. Shit—drunk panic attacks were way worse than sober ones. She staggered out of the toilet and barrelled straight into a chest. She gripped onto a firm arm and realised it was comfortably familiar.

'Let's go look at the sky,' the familiar voice said. Her hand was taken and she was blindly led from the club and out into the street.

It was better out here. Elise walked slowly, hand on her heart and eyes low on the pavement. She was led to a rail and gently pushed against it. Elise looked behind her. She was at the edge of the canal.

'Okay?' Cerulean asked.

Elise nodded. 'Went blind for a moment there.'

'But you see me now?'

'I see you.'

'Good. Waste of eyes if not.'

Elise blew out an amused breath. 'You're full of it. Where did you even come from tonight?'

Cerulean shook her head. 'Matters not when I'm from, only where I'm going.'

Elise leaned more heavily against the rail, slowly nodding to that. Weird. This girl was so weird. Her self-consciousness in shreds, Elise allowed herself to look over the girl in front of her. She was so buff and even in the dimness of night, Elise could see her tan. Didn't look fake either. And her face was nice. It always seemed smiley, even when it wasn't, and her eyes were crinkly around the edges like she spent her life squinting in the sun. And her smile…that was really, really nice.

'Thanks for rescuing me,' Elise said.

There was that smile. 'Not a problem.'

Elise shifted against the cold rail. She was having feelings right now. She ran her eyes over Cerulean's arms which were tensed where she had them crossed. They weren't the type of feelings straight girls had, either. Sometimes, she had dreams where she was attracted to girls. She'd wake up with the urge to go tell her sister that she was, actually, bi but as soon as the sleepiness dissipated, so did the feeling. She wondered if being drunk was a bit like that. But, she'd been drunk a couple of times before this and not felt even a hint of gay.

Elise blinked turned her eyes up to the sky. Maybe it was just the girl's muscles confusing her stupid, addled mind.

On a whim, she pulled out her phone and sent a text to Maddy. She wondered if she was still awake, carrying on the party with Phil. She still felt a bit bad that Maddy wasn't here, even if it was her own stupid fault.

'What do you wanna do?' she asked Cerulean, tucking away her phone.

'Walk with me?'

'Okay.' Elise pushed herself off the rail. 'Probably gonna get lost, though. I don't really know this city at night.'

'There's no such thing as lost when you're with another.'

Elise laughed. 'Alright then. In that case.'

They began their walk along the canal which was thronged with groups of people and the heavy base of club music.

'I don't often get to see the constellations,' Cerulean said.

Elise followed her gaze. She could see two, maybe three, stars up there. 'It's not great here in the city,' she said. 'It's better where I am, where it's more suburby. And it's *way* better out in the Peaks. Me and Maddy did a night hike out there once for school and oh my god.'

'The Peaks?'

'The Peak District. The national park between here and Sheffield. You know, lots of hills.'

'I've never been up a hill, only down.' When Elise laughed, Cerulean smiled and pushed on, 'Maybe you could take me there.'

'And force you up some hills?'

Cerulean nodded.

'Alright.' Her heart was thudding a bit harder. Had she just agreed to go on a date? Oops. She thought over that for a moment before deciding she didn't feel bad about it at all. 'It'll be freezing this time of year though.'

Cerulean grinned and shook her head. 'I burn from the inside out. Feel.'

Elise's hand was grabbed and hooked around a muscular arm. Cerulean was warm, despite being in short sleeves. Elise gave an experimental squeeze, smiling when Cerulean tensed deliberately and the muscle beneath her hand turned to rock.

'Can tell you work out,' she said.

'Physicality is important to me,' Cerulean agreed. 'There's power in it that's much underestimated. Especially by my sisters.'

'You have sisters?'

'Two of them.'

'Are you similar?'

Cerulean shook her head. 'Like night and day. Earlie and Risarial. I can't bear them most of the time.' Cerulean gave a smile which told Elise she was kidding. 'But alas, kin is kin.'

'Know the feeling.'

Cerulean looked at her. 'You do, don't you? It's true there's no one better suited to shoot you down, degrade you and love you like a sister.'

'Maddy's only bad some of the time,' Elise said defensively.

'And you are only good some of the time.'

She was teasing but Elise flushed anyway. 'How do you know?'

'I don't. Not so much. But I'd like to, if you'd let me.'

They reached a road bisecting the canal and slowed to a stop beneath a small tree. When Elise turned, Cerulean was very close.

'You have incredible eyes,' Elise said unthinkingly.

'As do you. As wide as moons.'

Why couldn't it be this way all the time? Words just slipping from her tongue, unfiltered and unfettered. It was so freeing. She was probably going to become an alcoholic after this, just to feel like this all the time. The thought made her giggle, forehead leaning forward and touching the top of Cerulean's arm.

'What's so funny?' Cerulean asked, cupping her head and pulling it away from her.

Elise ran a hand through her hair. 'Nothing.' She laughed gently again. 'I think I need to go home.'

That thought was a bit like a cold bucket of water. How would she even get home? The thought of getting a taxi back on her own was just *nope*. And—crap, she didn't have her house key.

But then Cerulean said, 'I will get you home, moon eyes,' and she felt her heart swell just a bit.

CHAPTER 13

Maddy pressed the home button on her phone for the billionth time, willing for a message to pop up.

'Dude, will you stop?' Phil said.

'I'm just checking. For Elise.'

'Is this *really* about Elise or do you just want that girl to message?'

Maddy shrugged. 'Both.'

They were sat on the sofa, their afterparty consisting of strong coffees and leftover snacks. Now that the normal lights were on, Maddy could see the mess left behind from the party—popped balloons, strewn playing cards and drink cans. Nothing seemed broken or stained though. Small mercies.

'Can't wait to tidy all this shit tomorrow,' she sighed.

'I'll help. Is it cool if I stop over again?'

Maddy nodded. 'Yeah. Spare room's still set up for you.'

'Cool.'

Maddy took a sip from her mug. 'Hey.'

'What?'

'We didn't bank the firepit.'

'Oh, shit.' Phil stood up and wandered through to the kitchen. 'It's out!' he called back. 'Someone else must have done it.'

'Or maybe we just did such a shit job of it that it went out on its own.'

'Well, the house didn't burn down so just be happy with

59

that.' He sat back down and narrowed his eyes at Maddy. 'You're in such a mood.'

'Am not. I'm just pissed.'

'Pissed *off*. We all told you a billion times to get your provisional sent off. You literally had an entire year.'

'Oh my god Phil, I know. I'm a massive failure. As always.'

'Woah. Hello, parent issues.' He took a slurp of his coffee. 'Dude, you met someone tonight, you should be happy.'

'Did I, though? We didn't even kiss. I'm not even sure she likes me back.'

'Well, you didn't really get the chance. Message her later on in the week, ask to meet up or something.'

'Maybe.'

'Hey, I need to tell you something.' Phil twisted to face her. 'You're gonna think I'm crazy but whatever.'

Maddy eyed him dubiously. 'What?'

'So, I went to the toilet earlier in Rainbows.'

'*Wow.*'

Phil grinned and hit her. 'Shut up. And in the toilets— and yeah, this is super fucked up—but they have a glory hole in one of the cubicles so you can see through into the girl's toilets.'

'What the fuck?'

'Yeah.' Phil shrugged. 'It's a gross place. And like, why would you want to see into the girl's toilets anyway? It's a *gay* bar. Anyway, because I'm a massive perv and there's nothing else to do when you're sat on the bog, I'm looking through it, right, and Cerulean comes in. And she goes into one of the cubicles—'

'Oh my god—you were watching all this?'

'Let me finish! So, she goes in and about five seconds later, all this light starts coming out of the cubicle. Like, under it and above it.'

Maddy frowned. 'What do you mean?'

'I don't know how else to explain it. Just *light*.'

'Maybe her phone torch?'

But Phil shook his head. 'No. It was bright, like sunshine bright. And then she flushed and the light went away and she came out and washed her hands, blah, blah, blah.'

Maddy found herself cackling heartily. 'So she glows when she shits. Love it.'

Phil sighed. 'I'm honestly not kidding. When I'm sober tomorrow, I'm gonna think about it more.'

Maddy patted him. 'Okay, you do that.'

'Anyway, I think I'm gonna go to bed. Are you?'

Maddy shook her head. 'Nah. Gonna try and wait up. I'm worried about Elise.'

'Why?'

Maddy sighed. 'She just gets panicky sometimes. And I know I rib her for it a lot, but she feels better when I go with her to things and I'm just worried she's gonna have a freak out at some point.'

'That's some twin co-dependency shit right there. You're adults now. She's gotta learn to live without you at some point.'

'Suppose.'

Phil stood. 'Night then.'

'Yeah, night.'

When Maddy next checked the time, an hour had passed, an hour where she'd done nothing but stare at the empty fireplace in front of her, thinking about Cerulean and the rest of her birthday. But mostly Cerulean.

Her phone finally pinged at around half two, but it was from Elise, not Cerulean, and it read, *I like your friend. She's actually kind of attractive for a girl xxx*

Maddy stared at the text for a moment too long, her insides doing something weird, like boiling up and turning to steam.

What the fuck??? she finally messaged back.

She got no reply.

Maddy must have fallen asleep after that because the next thing she knew, she was waking up with her head pillowed on the arm of the chair, and her phone vibrating in her clenched hands. Cerulean was ringing her. She sat up groggily and cleared her throat.

'Hey. You okay?'

'All is well. I am at your front door. I have your sister.'

Maddy's head turned in the direction of the door. 'Oh, okay. One sec.'

Maddy staggered as she stood up and crossed to the hall. She unlocked the door and pulled it open, expecting her sister to be passed out and being carried or something. But she didn't look too worse for wear, even if Cerulean was supporting her with an arm around her waist.

Elise smiled. 'Hey, Mads.'

'Hey.' Maddy stepped back. 'Good night?'

'Super good, thanks. Need to sleep now.'

'Okay. I'll get you some water first. You'll be hungover as hell otherwise.'

Maddy left Cerulean in the lounge as she poured Elise a glass of water and commanded her to drink it.

'Did you really have a good time?' she asked quietly.

Elise nodded, heartily drinking the water.

Maddy left her there and returned to Cerulean.

'Hey, do you live around here?' When Cerulean shook her head, she said, 'Okay. Wanna stop over? We don't have any spare rooms tonight but you're free to take the sofa. It's comfy.'

Cerulean smiled. 'I would like that.'

'Cool. Bathroom's just at the top of the stairs if you need it.' She teased, 'And again, no stealing anything.'

When Elise had finished her water, Maddy poured her another and then prodded her up the stairs to her bedroom.

'Lie down.'

Elise didn't need to be told twice. She quickly shrugged out of her dress and tights and into her pyjamas before burying herself under the covers.

'*Brrr,*' she shivered. 'I don't think I'm ever going to be warm again.'

'I'll put the heating on for a bit.' Maddy stood at the edge of the bed and looked over her sister, feeling a strange swelling of something akin to disappointment. Had she wanted Elise to have a bad night without her? 'Dude, you look like a panda. What the fuck have you done to your makeup?'

With her eyes closed, Elise smiled. 'You're so mean to me. But I love you.'

Maddy chuckled. 'Shut up. God, you're going to have such a hangover tomorrow.'

Elise screwed up her face and let out a faux sob. 'I know.'

Maddy walked over to the window to close the curtains, catching sight of tree branches swaying beneath the streetlamps. 'Hey, Ellie-Wellie?'

'Hey, Laddy-Maddy.'

'Actually, it's more Saddy-Maddy these days.'

'Cheer up, dick. It's our birthday. What?'

Maddy sat down on the bed. 'Why have you hidden one of my t-shirts and a pack of cigs in a plastic bag in the woods?' No response. 'Elise?'

'I can't answer. I've passed out.'

Maddy snorted. 'Fine. Keep your secrets, freak. Want me to get you a sick bucket?'

'No thanks. I'll take my chances.'

Maddy stood up and hit the lights. 'Okay. Bye.'

Just as she stepped out of the room, Elise's asked quietly, 'Is Cerulean still here?'

'Yeah. Kipping on the sofa.'

A pause. 'Cool.'

Maddy rolled her eyes and left the room, pulling the door shut a little too hard.

CHAPTER 14

Maddy hovered over the toilet for another ten seconds before deciding she wasn't going to be sick. She blew out a piteous breath and slowly made her way downstairs. It was just past ten in the morning and the early light poured through the patio doors of the kitchen like knives through her forehead. The house was quiet; no one else seemed to be up.

The kitchen was a tip. With a sigh, Maddy opened the cupboard under the sink and pulled out a roll of bin bags. She should probably eat first but her stomach was doing weird things and she didn't trust herself to keep anything down right now.

She had just started bagging up the empty cans from the table when she spotted a pair of bare feet propped up on the arm of the sofa.

Oh. She'd almost forgotten.

She ducked out of view and used the edge of a finger to wipe off as much smeared eye makeup as she could. She looked down at herself. She was only dressed in a t-shirt. It was baggy enough to be labelled a dress but still left her legs totally bare. And her hair—it was just a mess. After a moment, Maddy shrugged. Oh well.

She walked into the lounge.

'Hey.'

Cerulean smiled. She was clutching the blanket to her chest and one muscular arm was tucked beneath her head.

''Morning,' she said, her voice all gravelly with sleep. The sound of it shot right through Maddy.

'Feeling okay?'

Cerulean nodded. 'And you?'

Maddy tilted her head. 'Kinda. Been worse.' Cerulean closed her eyes again. 'Hey, thanks for coming to the party last night. Even if you did crash it.'

'No problem.'

Maddy hovered there for a moment, then took a breath. 'So, don't suppose you fancy—'

'Morning!'

Maddy looked up. Elise was descending the stairs a little too perkily, hair pulled off her face in a messy bun and wearing shorts and a long-sleeved top which hid her hands.

Cerulean craned her neck to see. 'Good morning.'

As soon as Elise reached her, Maddy thrust a bin bag at her. 'Here. Help me.' She pulled her into the kitchen. 'Nice to see you're alive.'

'I don't feel so bad, actually.'

'It'll hit you later,' Maddy said. 'Always does me.'

'Probably.'

Elise kept looking through to the lounge as she cleaned and it pissed Maddy off. 'Will you stop?' she snapped.

'Stop what?'

'Perving.'

Elise gave her a look but said nothing.

When they started on the lounge, Cerulean was still lying there. She'd pulled one of the paper snack plates onto her chest and was slowly eating Hula Hoops, taking them off the tips of her fingers with her teeth, one by one.

They'd just finished bagging everything away, mostly in silence, when Phil finally made his appearance. Seeing that they'd done most of the work already, he said, 'I'll run the hoover around, guys.'

Maddy threw him a grateful smile then took the bags out to the bin. When she returned, Cerulean was up, bag slung over her shoulder, and putting on her boots.

'Are you going?' Maddy asked.

Cerulean nodded. 'Thank you for your hospitality.'

'You're welcome,' Elise answered. She stood against the wall with folded arms, ready to walk Cerulean to the door, something that really bloody annoyed Maddy. 'Thanks for making sure I got home safely.'

Cerulean flashed her a smile. 'My pleasure. Always.'

The two disappeared into the hall and Maddy stood there like an idiot, listening to them talking softly.

Next to her, Phil bunched his eyebrows together and threw a thumb towards the front door. 'Dude, are those two...?' Maddy gave an exaggerated shrug. 'But I thought Elise was straight.'

'So did I.'

Phil laughed. 'Oh shit. This is so bad.'

'It is so fucking bad,' Maddy agreed.

She heard the front door shut. When Elise came back into the lounge, she tucked a strand of hair behind her ear and said a little awkwardly, 'She's nice.'

'She could've helped us tidy the place,' Maddy countered. 'She just sat there!'

'I dunno,' Elise said slowly, folding her arms around herself, 'I thought she looked kind of hot just draped like that.'

Maddy snorted in disgust. 'Wow, absolute bare minimum. You are so fucking *straight*.'

'Actually, I'm reconsidering that.'

'Don't be that guy, Elise. One drunken crush on a girl who looks like a boy does not make you gay.'

'I'm not drunk now.' Elise yawned widely, then shook her head out. 'Just really hungover so stop having a go. We've cleaned. I'm going back to bed.'

When Elise had ascended out of sight, Maddy dug the heels of her hands into her eyes and groaned loudly.

'Hey,' Phil said in a wheedling voice, sidling up to her, 'can I make myself a fried egg sandwich?'

'Do what you want,' Maddy said, starting up the stairs

after her sister. 'I'm going back to bed too.'

CHAPTER 15

Three days later, Maddy and Elise returned from college to a doorway full of Christmas tree. Maddy craned her neck to see her Mum's face looming up behind it.

When she saw the two of them, she gave a harried smile. 'Give me a hand will you girls?'

'What the hell, Mum?' Maddy scooted around the tree, batting piney branches away from her face. 'Bit early, isn't it?'

'It's almost December. That Christmas tree place up at the park just opened. Couldn't resist as I drove past.'

'Where's Dad?' Elise asked. She'd squeezed past and stood watching against the hallway wall as the tree was pulled further into the house.

'He's staying on for a bit but I felt bad leaving you girls for so long. He'll be back in a few days. Into the lounge, Mads.'

'I know where to put it.'

With Elise's help, the three of them rightened the tree into its base, the wood flooring already strewn with pine needles.

Hastily, her mum fluffed the branches back into order. 'Right. I'll get the box from the loft and we can get this thing decorated.'

'Now?' Elise asked dubiously.

'Yes, now. And as we do, you two can tell me all about your birthday.' She gave them each a kiss on the cheek before jogging up the stairs.

Maddy followed her with her eyes. 'How much do you wanna bet she'll ditch us in five minutes?'

Elise sighed. 'Don't, Maddy.'

'What?'

'Nothing. Let's just do what she wants. I don't want a fight.'

'Me neither! What—where does a fight come into this?'

Lips pressed together, Elise shook her head, reaching past Maddy to fiddle with one of the branches.

When her mum returned a few minutes later and dropped a drooping cardboard box at her feet, Maddy was in a mood. There was no reason for it exactly, except that things were always a bit tense when their parents came back from one of their extended work trips.

'God, I need a glass of wine,' her mum said. 'Hey, you girls want one too? Now that you're both adults. *God*, I can't believe you two are eighteen.'

'I'm good,' Maddy replied.

'Same,' said Elise.

Wine poured, her mum leant against the back of the sofa, watching them dig around in the box through large, black framed glasses. Her hair was short and blonde, framing her face with a gentle wave. She looked every bit like the scientist nerd that she was. Maddy pulled out an almost thread-bare snake of tinsel; the green one she knew her mum hated.

'Oh Mads, not that ratty thing,' came the complaint she wanted but she'd already reached up and slung it around the tree. At her feet, Elise shook her head but Maddy spotted a tiny smile on her face.

'So girls, how was your birthday? Did you have the party in the end?'

'Yeah, it was good,' Elise replied.

'Good. Glad to see the house is still in one piece. Did you both get the money me and Dad put in your accounts?'

'Yep,' they answered in unison.

'Good.' After another few minutes of silence, her mum pushed off from the sofa. 'Right, well I need to type up a report and send it off to the university. I said I'd get it done by tonight. If you two need me, I'll be in the office.'

'Wow,' Maddy said, once she'd heard the office door shut above them. 'Just under ten minutes there. And she actually *asked* about us.'

Elise snorted softly. 'Yeah.'

Maddy dropped the bauble she was holding and stepped away from the tree. 'This is dumb.'

'Hey.' Elise whirled on her. 'Don't make me do this alone. Please.'

Blowing out a raspberry, Maddy returned to the box. 'Fine. But it's still dumb.'

'You're dumb.'

Maddy snorted. 'Wow. Sure you're eighteen?'

'I'm sure. Hey, actually I need to ask you a favour.'

'Mm-hm?'

With a paper angel in hand—some crappy thing Maddy made when she was six—Elise sat back on her heels, one hand reaching up to tuck a strand of hair behind her ear. 'I was wondering if you could give me Cerulean's number?'

'Why?'

Elise raised her eyebrows. 'So I can message her?'

'Yeah, but why?'

'What do you mean, *why?* I just want to talk to her. Don't be a dick, Maddy.'

'She's gay.'

'I know that.'

'And you're not. So why do you want to get involved with her? That's kind of shitty, Elise. God, you straight girls are all the same.'

Elise frowned. 'That's not it.' She swivelled to face her sister. 'Maddy, tell me honestly—did something happen between the two of you that night? She was in your room…'

Yes! Maddy desperately wanted to say. *Yes, it did.* But that wasn't true and the fact it wasn't pissed Maddy off all the more. 'No, nothing happened. Literally nothing. We just talked and then we went out.'

'Okay,' Elise said quietly. 'Good. So, I don't have to feel bad if…'

'Elise!' Maddy let out an exasperated breath. 'You are not *into girls*.'

'Well, I'm into this one.' She said this quietly but there was a sense of finality to her tone which sent Maddy into a strange panic. 'Please can I just have her number?'

Maddy looked at Elise, at her clear face and wide, brown eyes. God, did Maddy really look like that too? So young and stupid-looking. She hated it. She dyed her hair and put way too much eyeliner on and wore nothing but black and she still hated it.

'Fine.' She pulled her college bag to her, fished out her phone and tossed it to Elise. 'Here.'

As she sat there, watching Elise copy Cerulean's number into her phone surrounded by Christmas decorations, Maddy wanted to cry.

Before she could let herself do that, she stood up. 'You can finish the tree.'

☙❧

Maddy knew she'd regret giving Elise Cerulean's number but she hadn't thought she'd regret it so quickly. She also hadn't thought Elise would make the dick move of not hiding the fact that she was texting Cerulean every second of every day. Maddy wished beyond anything that she'd messaged Cerulean first instead of doing the not-acting-too-keen thing. Every bloody decision she made was always the wrong one.

It was worse in English, where the two sat next to each other and Maddy couldn't escape to her room or piss off to the park with Phil. Maddy always took the mick out of Elise for being so attentive in class—*gormy* was her preferred adjective—but this was worse, way worse. Elise didn't pay attention to a thing, eyes low on her lap as she tapped out message after message.

Maddy tried not to look, she really did, but it was like someone else was commanding her eyes. She saw winking faces and hearts and wanted to puke.

Afterwards, Phil found her in the corridor. 'Hey,' he said. 'We're all off to Poundland. Apparently they sell vibrators now, like what the fuck? You wanna come?'

'No,' Maddy said, watching Elise disappear into a throng of students. 'I'm going to the pub.'

'Oh. I mean, I'd rather do that.'

'Let's go then.'

When they got to the pub, a tiny, dingy place in the centre of town, something reckless came over Maddy and she ordered them shots instead of pints. They only had an hour before Photography but fuck it.

'*O-kay*,' Phil said as she slammed them down in front of him. Maddy was only thankful he at least had the decency to ask her what was wrong *after* they downed the shots.

'Elise is having it off with Cerulean,' Maddy said, enjoying the cherry-flavoured burn in her mouth.

'Having it off?'

'I mean, they're messaging all the time and it's driving me mad.'

'Just ignore it.'

'I *can't.*'

'Well—' Phil blew out a breath. 'You're gonna have to distract yourself or something then. Go meet up with someone else—anyone else. Look, you tried with Cerulean and she didn't bite and now she likes your sister for some reason. Who's now suddenly a lesbian. It's shit but it's fine.'

Maddy dropped her head onto her fist. 'If you were a lesbian, would you rather date me or Elise?'

Phil pursed his lips. 'Toughie. I love you the most but Elise has her shit together more than you do.'

Maddy snorted. 'No she fucking doesn't. Thanks Phil. That makes me feel great.'

'Hey, you asked. Just because she's not interested, doesn't mean other girls won't be. How's the online thing going?'

Maddy shrugged. There had been a few girls she'd matched with, some pretty fit ones too, but her brain was filled with that stupid, curly-haired—

'Just go meet one. You never know.'

'Yeah. Maybe.' She glanced at the bar. 'Want some more?'

'Some *more?* Dude.'

'Fine.' Maddy stood up. 'Just for me then.'

CHAPTER 16

Elise watched the snow fluttering from her bedroom window, sweating in her winter coat and scarf. The snow was meant to have stopped—the weather app said it would stop. Elise drummed her fingers on the windowsill, taking deep, silent breaths against the rapid beating of her heart.

She checked the time on her phone again. Almost time.

She'd been ready for ages and spent the last half an hour checking that her makeup hadn't smudged, that her coat would cover her bum and not show her knicker line, that she had her phone, purse and house key on her. She honestly couldn't be more ready.

When it was time, Elise left her room and came to stand in Maddy's open doorway. Her sister was on her bed, laptop on lap with a plate of toast crusts on the pillow beside her.

Spotting her, Maddy frowned. 'Where are you going?'

Elise took a breath. '*Sooo*, I'm going to see Cerulean.'

Maddy looked away. 'Okay. Why are you telling me?'

Elise frowned. 'I don't know actually.'

'Trying to rub it in?'

'No!' Elise sighed and turned away. 'Never mind.'

'Wait. Elise, it's snowing. Is it really a good idea to go traipsing around in the Peaks now?'

'I know what this is about,' Elise said slowly, 'and it's nothing to do with the snow.'

Maddy blew out a breath and Elise braced herself. 'It's just—this literally never happens to me. I actually meet someone I like and—why her, Elise? You're so pretty and nice, you could literally have anyone you wanted. Why *her*? Why someone I was interested in first?'

'Maddy, you're acting like I planned for this to happen. And *nothing* happened between the two of you. You said. You don't have any claim on her so stop pretending that you do.'

Maddy shoved the laptop away from her. 'Fuck's sake. All because I didn't send off for my fucking provisional!'

'Oh give over, Maddy.'

Maddy sighed. She looked at Elise, at the way her hands fiddled with the gloves she hadn't put on yet and asked, 'You nervous?'

Elise released a trembling breath. 'Yeah.'

'It'll be fine,' she said dismissively. 'Have fun.'

Elise loitered for a moment. 'Thanks. See you later.'

The snow had barely settled on her street but she walked to the bus stop slowly in case of ice. She knew it would be a different matter in the Peaks. Maddy was right, it probably wasn't wise to go, but Elise was kind of over being wise. Despite her nerves, she was looking forward to seeing Cerulean again. They'd talked—a lot—though only over text and the occasional call. Something about video calling sent Elise into an anxious spiral, but thankfully Cerulean never asked.

She didn't quite feel like herself as she boarded the bus. This happened a lot when she did something outside of her honed routine—her mind would sort of shut down and draw away from itself until she felt like she was in a dream. She knew it was some kind of trauma response but it had been going on since she was a kid and she was pretty sure she was beyond help.

As soon as she got off the bus, the nerves set in again. She'd arranged to meet Cerulean outside the train station and she walked there slowly, eyes flitting over the entrance until she spotted her sitting on a bollard. Elise's heart jumped. She had a hat on, crushing her blonde curls, but her jacket didn't look suitable for this kind of weather. It was boxy and made up in patchwork colours.

She gave a wave when Cerulean's eyes met hers and she felt her own lips quirk at the warm smile Cerulean graced her with.

'Hi,' Elise said as she neared her.

'Hello.'

'Are you not cold?' Elise asked, briefly reaching out to touch the sleeve of Cerulean's jacket.

Cerulean shook her head. 'No, I told you—I burn internally.'

'Cool.' Elise glanced at the train station behind them. 'Well, shall we…?'

Cerulean nodded her on.

'We've got about ten minutes before the train.' Elise glanced back to make sure Cerulean was following her. 'Do you want any food or anything?' She gestured to the kiosks around them. When Cerulean shook her head, she went on, 'Okay. I brought a couple of things for us. You know, if we get hungry.'

'That is good thinking.' Cerulean ducked her head. 'I did not think ahead.'

Elise waved her off. 'It's cool. I think too much sometimes.'

The train was already waiting at the platform and they boarded, claiming a table with four seats around it. Elise squeezed into one side, Cerulean the other.

'And this will get to where we're going?' Cerulean asked, eyeing the carriage. She took off her hat and wrung it between her hands.

'Yep. It's about forty minutes.'

'Incredible.'

Cerulean reached up and ran her fingers through her hat-flattened hair. Elise watched her finish the avid inspection of the train before she turned her eyes onto her. Under the attention, Elise flushed, squeezing her fingers together so she wouldn't fidget.

When Cerulean's smile turned warm, sly almost, Elise asked, 'What?'

'I'm surprised you have it in you to move at all, bundled up in all those layers.'

Elise smiled. 'Shut up. I'm cold. Not everyone gets to be a furnace like you.'

Cerulean only smiled and held out her hand. Elise put her gloved one in it, unable to look away as the glove was slowly removed and her hand cradled between two of Cerulean's.

'Your blood—it runs like ice through your veins.'

'I don't know,' Elise whispered. 'It's kind of warming up now.'

Elise was aware of a couple claiming the table seat beside them but she tried to pay them no mind as Cerulean lifted her hand to her mouth and began blowing hot air onto it. Her eyes were rapt on Elise's and Elise, knowing full well that she was being outrageously flirted with, couldn't look away. Cerulean turned Elise's hand over and then pressed her lips to the middle of her palm and a bolt shot straight to the point between her legs.

Now Elise shifted on her seat. That was bloody new. No girl had ever elicited that sensation in her before. No boy either, for that matter.

With a last crooked smile, Cerulean released her hand and sat back as the train began rolling out of the station. They didn't talk much during the journey. Cerulean seemed content to peer out the window and Elise didn't want to converse with so many people pressed around her.

This journey was always a nice one, especially when the train emerged from the city and into the countryside. The clouds hung low today, thickly obscuring the snow-capped hills. Elise couldn't even see the skyline she had planned on walking around.

They were the only two to get off at their stop, a testament to just how rubbish the weather was.

Elise blew out a breath at how much colder and windier

it was here but Cerulean seemed completely non-plussed, following the train with her eyes as it sped off.

'So much fresher than the city,' she commented.

'Yeah, it's pretty nice out here.'

To her amusement, Cerulean proceeded to raise her head and stick the tip of her tongue out. 'What are you doing?' Elise asked.

'Tastes fresher too.' She gestured to the dusting of snow on the verge. 'This—this snow, it's almost sweet.'

Elise pursed her lips. Cerulean was still weird then, even sober. As a rule, Elise innately dislike anyone with a distinct cringe factor. It honestly just hurt her to witness but with Cerulean...

'Are you ready for a hill?'

Cerulean chuckled. 'Yes. Make it hurt.'

Feeling brave, Elise hooked her arm around Cerulean's. 'Careful what you wish for,' she said.

The way up wasn't too horrendous, at least not snow-wise. The trail was mostly hardpacked earth, shadowed by boulders which took the brunt of the snow, leaving the path protected. Elise was pretty agile but she wasn't above accepting Cerulean's hand as they jumped from the bigger boulders.

'This terrain is unforgiving,' Cerulean commented as they peaked the first incline. Out of the protection of the valley, the wind was relentless and they had to shout to hear.

'Do you hate it?'

Cerulean shook her head. 'Far from.'

When the wind lessened slightly, she said, 'So, what do you do?'

'Do?'

'Yeah, like for a job or whatever.'

'I see. Well, I don't have one of those. I am a mere traveller.'

'Oh. Where do you come from then?'

'Not too far away. Probably not a place you're familiar with. My sister—both of them actually—recommended this place. Sent me this way.'

Elise nodded. 'Well, I'm glad they did.' She caught Cerulean's fingers and squeezed them, her heart beating a crazed rhythm at how bold she was being. 'I'm super glad I met you.'

It was the truth. She felt better than she had in forever. She felt almost alive, a far cry from her usual emotional nothingness. The wind burnt her eyes and the snow was rapidly deepening but her heart soared at the sheer pleasure of being with Cerulean, with someone who liked her this way. It was mad, really. Apart from one drunken night and a smattering of text messages, she barely knew the girl but she knew, hand on her heart, there was no place she'd rather be than traversing this ridgeline and no person she'd rather be with than this buff, blonde-haired weirdo.

They were almost at the top. Conversation ground to a halt as the wind and cold grew too fierce to do anything more than carefully place one booted foot in front of the other. Cerulean had a grip of Elise permanently now and Elise was more than happy to just let her lead, revelling in this thing tingling between them.

The snow was deep in parts, the path almost completely obscured. This was probably super dangerous but Elise tried to ignore that nagging side of her brain. They skirted around a particularly high snowdrift which Elise was sure was where the actual path was meant to be. Instead, they walked on crunchy, snow-beaten heather and trampled grass.

'Easy,' Cerulean said into her ear, gripping her arm tighter.

Elise smiled her thanks just as her foot fell straight through into an icy puddle of water. She cried out, latching onto Cerulean who pulled her free. Elise heard laughing very close to her face.

'It's not funny,' Elise chuckled, breathlessly. 'It's bloody freezing.'

It actually really wasn't funny; the water had flooded her boot and trouser leg and they were about an hour away from the valley floor now. Elise sighed. She was in for a majorly uncomfortable hike. She could almost hear Maddy's *I told you so*.

'Come on,' Cerulean said. 'Let's go back to that stone cluster over there.'

Slowly, they trekked back to the last outcropping of boulders. If it wasn't for the freezing seeping of her foot, Elise would have had a great time with Cerulean walked methodically around the boulders, sizing each of them up carefully like she was surveying for a home to buy.

'Over here,' she said quietly and Elise smiled, latching onto the hand that was offered to her.

They were on the edge of the hill, overlooking the white, vast countryside. Cerulean found a little nook in the rocks which enclosed three sides of them, apart from the view, and helped Elise up into it.

'Cosy,' she said, teeth chattering.

They were sheltered from the wind entirely and the sudden silence was almost loud. Cerulean squeezed in beside her, pulling herself right to the back of the nook so Elise was almost sitting back against her chest.

God, it was all so intimate suddenly. Elise's heart was jackhammering and there was a stirring somewhere lower too. She thought the heat washing over her was from her own fluster but it wasn't—it was pouring off Cerulean in waves.

Elise found Cerulean's eyes in the dim. 'God, the heat of you,' she breathed.

Cerulean reached out and cupped her face. 'Yes,' she murmured. 'The heat of me.'

Then, warm, silky lips were on hers and Elise's eyes slammed shut. There was no movement to their mouths, just one, firm press which Elise stiffened to completely, breath stuttering to a halt. It shouldn't have surprised her, they were on a *date*, but it did and it was glorious. Elise was so rarely shocked by anything, a condition of living as surely and as carefully as she did.

When her mind finally caught up and began to chatter, she pressed forward, hands coming to Cerulean's shoulders, desperate to smother it.

Cerulean pulled away, just slightly, and looked down at her sodden leg. 'Now, let's sort this out shall we.'

One large, golden hand came to the top of her boot and Elise couldn't do anything more than sit there and watch as her foot and trouser leg dried right in front of her eyes.

Cerulean's hand was now in Elise's hair, stroking reverently. 'There,' she whispered. 'Bet that feels much better, hm?'

Elise let out a breath. 'How—?' She shook her head. 'What did you just do?'

Cerulean chuckled. 'Dried you. Well, your foot at least.'

Elise turned around so she could face Cerulean and for the first time, looked at her properly, without shyness, without any reserve at all. Cerulean stared back steadily and Elise felt—not scared exactly, but there was an awareness that something else was going on beneath the surface here. Something big. Elise turned back around, snared by the whiteness in front of her. Maybe something too big.

Cerulean moved the hair she was stroking to the side and pressed her lips to her neck. Elise closed her eyes.

'Elise?'

'Mm?'

Another kiss to her neck. 'Your heart—I can feel it beating like a bird's wing. When it slows, I will be here.'

Elise took a breath and half turned back to face her. 'I'm not sure I want it to slow.'

It was mad, really, that the only response she had to all of that was to kiss the girl again.

❧ ❦

Maddy had heard Elise arrive home half an hour ago but refused to seek her out straight away, not wanting to give her the satisfaction. But finally, she couldn't wait anymore.

She knocked on her bedroom door, waiting for the muffled *what?* before pushing it open. She frowned—Elise was still in her coat, lying outstretched on her bed, one arm above her head.

'Um, are you okay?'

Elise nodded slowly. 'Mm-hm.'

Maddy's eyes travelled around the room before landing back on her sister who hadn't even glanced at her yet.

'So, did you have a good time or what?'

'Very good,' Elise whispered.

Maddy stared for another moment before finally blurting, 'Did you sleep with her?'

This at least roused Elise. 'What? No! Why would you even ask that?'

Maddy shrugged. 'I dunno. You're acting kind of weird and your eyes are all like,' Maddy waved a hand in front of her own face, 'glazed over.'

Elise went back to staring at the ceiling. 'I'm fine. I promise. I'm just—thinking.'

'Okay. Whatever. I'll leave you to your thinking.'

Maddy closed the door, feeling a jumble of emotions she couldn't even begin to pick out, though she knew none of them were good. She had the mad urge to text Cerulean, to ask her—god, she didn't even know what. This sucked, this really fucking sucked, and she didn't know why it sucked so much, only that it really fucking did.

She went back to her own room and fished out her phone, scrolling past Cerulean's number until she got to Phil's.

Rainbows at 8? I need to get drunk so bad.

❧ ❧

'You, my guy, are turning into a raging alchy.'

With a grin, Maddy accepted the two bottles of alcopop Phil held out for her. 'Yeah well, I'm dragging you down with me.'

'You always drag me down.' Phil plopped down on the booth beside her. '*Soooo*, you gonna tell me what's gone on?'

Maddy took a long sip of her drink, idly watching two middle-aged women dancing in front of the vacant DJ booth. 'Elise went out on a date with Cerulean earlier.'

'Ah.'

'I think it went well.'

'And…what, you're not happy about that?'

'Of course I'm bloody not.'

Phil dropped his head back and let out a loud groan. 'Maddy, you *have* to let this go.'

'How? Phil—I know it might seem like I'm crazy, like I'm obsessing or whatever—'

'You are.'

'—But I'm telling you, there was something there at the night of the party. There was. And then afterwards, her and Elise went off to Manchester and I don't know, I guess something happened. But she was into me *first*, I'm telling you. She winked at me so many times.'

'Yeah but—' Phil sighed. 'She's not now. She's into Elise—which I get, sucks—but you're gonna have to get over it. Especially if they end up in a relationship.'

Maddy lips twisted. 'Urgh.'

'Maddy, please for the love of god, just meet up with someone else. Hey, think about it this way. Do you really want your twin sister—your *straight* twin sister—to lose her lesbian v-card before you?'

Silently, Maddy shook her head.

'Thought not. Here, give me your phone. I'm gonna find someone for you right now.'

Almost desperately, Maddy handed over her phone, watching over Phil's shoulder as he swiped through the various options. None of them appealed to her, literally not one, but by the end of the hour, she'd matched with a few of them and Phil had sent out a couple of *hi*'s.

She was pretty tipsy by the time she got home. She would have stayed out for longer but Phil reminded her that they had college in the morning, the bore. She fell onto her bed, hastily reaching out to catch her phone before it bounced to the floor. She saw a notification from the dating site on her home screen and blew out a loud raspberry before opening it.

Chloe: Hi back :) How are you?

Maddy rolled her eyes to the ceiling. Why was everyone so bloody boring?

Still, she found herself replying, if only because Phil's earlier words came back to haunt her with a vengeance. He was right—there was no way that *she*, an *actual* lesbian, was going to have sex with a girl *after* her straight-as-fuck virgin sister. Just no way.

She tapped to the girl's profile and swiped through her pictures. She was pretty hot. Didn't have short hair but wasn't too feminine either. She was a couple of years older than Maddy but that was cool too.

When the girl next replied, Maddy felt a bit more interested.

Chloe: Yeah, I'm doing good too ta. So going by our profiles, it looks like we're after the same thing, a.k.a nothing haha

Maddy smiled. So the girl was only after casual too. Fabulous. A pressure eased off her chest.

Maddy: Haha yeah, looks like. Good to know we're on the same page :)

Chloe's next message had her heart beating a little harder: *Do you want to meet?*

Maddy bit her lip. Did she? Kind of not really, but also…Slowly, she typed back, *Yeah, that would be cool. When?*

After she'd sent it, she pulled a pillow onto her face and kept it there, enjoying the coolness of it against her burning cheeks.

CHAPTER 17

Cerulean stood at the window of her hotel room, one forearm against the cool glass, the other holding a bottle of beer. She took a sip, licking the wheaty liquid from her lips, idly watching the humans scuttling below.

She'd chosen a hotel right in the centre of Manchester, a luxury, glass-encased gargantuan building. Eyeing the sponge-smeared window before her, Cerulean thought the humans held an interesting idea of the word 'luxury'.

No matter, she at least had a bowl of something being cooked up by the hotel staff.

Just as a knock came to the door, her phone began ringing. Cerulean glanced at its screen as she crossed the carpet and grinned, recognising the number.

Giving a nod to the man on the other side of the door, she wheeled in her food and put the phone to her ear.

'Sister!'

'Cerulean.' Risarial's smooth, low voice drifted to her through the phone.

Cerulean dropped down on the bed, pulling the tray towards her. 'How bizarre—us talking like this.'

'Quite.'

She picked up a spoon and slurped some of the soup she'd ordered. It was swimming with noodles and bits of spring onion. 'Where are you then?'

'Atop the hill.' A tremulous sigh. 'It is cold tonight.'

Cerulean pictured her oldest sister perched on some

fallen, crumbling log, a furrow in her brow, her face a perpetual mask of dark, dour beauty.

'Pah! You are like the humans. So shivery and brittle.' There were brown bits beneath the nest of noodles. Cerulean prodded at them curiously. 'The food here—it's quite different from home, is it not? I would never have thought—noodles! We must have the kitchens try it. I think dough is all that's needed, and something to turn it to ribbons. And there are claggy things called dumplings—'

'Cerulean. I'm not calling about the food.'

Cerulean gave a low chuckle. 'I know what you're calling about. You wish me to reveal all my secrets.'

'You have some then.'

'I believe so, I believe so.' Cerulean paused, lowering the spoon. 'There is someone—'

'Only the one?'

'Yes, well, after separating the wheat from the chaff, it seems to have come down to one.'

'Do tell.'

Cerulean pursed her lips. 'No, I don't think I shall.'

'Cerulean.'

'It is new, Risarial! A fragile thing. She is a fragile thing.' Cerulean let out a chuckle of derision. 'Although, I fear I may have betrayed our kind to her.' She shrugged, though her sister couldn't see. 'I admit to showing off.'

'You always were a gloat.'

Cerulean nodded. 'Unabashedly.' In fact, her most favourite thing to do was visit public toilets, secure herself behind the door and let her glamour slip from her. There was something gratifying in letting the brightness of herself shine in such a dank, dirty place. It was—truly—only a matter of time before she was discovered. Heavens, but what fun.

'I have a feeling though,' she went on, tapping the back of the spoon against her lips, 'it wasn't so much a mistake.'

'I hope for your sake it was not. It is a good thing this fragile human won't remember you by the end.'

It was a thinly veiled warning. Cerulean rolled her eyes. 'Don't be a bore. I've only just gotten started here, Risarial. I cannot even think of giving it up yet.'

'And I won't ask you to. Yet.' Risarial sighed. 'I can't bear this chill any longer. I must go.'

'Go then, sister. Leave me be.'

A pause. 'Just…use caution, Cerulean. Guard yourself. Guard your heart.'

'Goodbye, Risarial.'

Cerulean hung up. She flung the phone onto the bed behind her and pulled her bowl of soup fully into her lap.

Telling her to guard her heart when she was here to fulfil a *love* bargain was just so very Risarial. Cerulean shook her head. There was no danger to be had here. Here, she was the apex. The one who shone like the sun, the one who could glamour anyone to lick her boots or force them into servitude for the rest of their tiny lives, making her noodles and dumplings until she was sick of them. Cerulean grinned to herself. Not that she would, of course.

She thought back to her date the other day, remembering with glee all that white, rolling countryside, the height of it and the roaring wind at the summit. The girl she was with. Cerulean sipped from her spoon absently. Elise seemed quieter than the rest, reserved and locked-in, even when she had imbibed on the night of her name day. It was true Cerulean liked a challenge but there was something more intriguing than that about Elise, something she couldn't quite put her finger on yet. But she would.

CHAPTER 18

Maddy stepped into the pub and hovered near the door, scanning the interior. It was a nice pub and not one she'd ever been to before. Kind of student-y with lots of stylish exposed brick and neon lighting.

'Maddy!'

Maddy's head snapped to the left, where Chloe sat at a booth, a pint of something on the table before her. Maddy took a breath and started towards her.

'Hey.'

Chloe smiled. Under the nude bulb on the wall beside her, her long, straightened hair was impossibly glossy.

'Hi.' She nodded towards her pint. 'Sorry. Didn't know what you wanted.'

Maddy shrugged off her bag and tossed it onto the bench. 'That's cool. Be right back.'

Purse in hand, she headed to the bar and ordered a bottle of berry cider. She removed her card reluctantly; it was expensive as hell here.

As the bartender poured from the bottle into a glass for her, Maddy glanced back to Chloe who had her head down, rapidly typing on her phone. She was just as attractive as her photos, thank god. Kinda boyish, but pretty too, with a slightly stern expression and eyes as dark as her own.

'How was your bus ride here?' Chloe asked when she'd gotten settled.

'Yeah. Okay. Not too busy thankfully.' Maddy rubbed at

the condensation left by her glass on the table, waiting for the jiggling nerves inside her to settle. 'How about you? Do you live close?'

'Closer than you, just outside of the city centre.'

'You're at Manchester Met, aren't you. First year?'

'No. Second.'

'Cool. I might be studying there next year.'

Chloe tilted her head. 'Wait, so you're still at sixth form then, or college?'

'Yeah, college. Just turned eighteen last month.'

'Ah.' Chloe nodded. 'Sweet.' She picked up her pint and took a long sip from it, doing that thing lesbians do where they lifted their elbow up higher than necessary. Maddy didn't know why it was hot, but it was. She put down her glass again and said, 'So you're just after casual, right?'

Maddy nodded. 'Kinda, yeah.'

'*Sooo*,' she ran a fingertip around the rim of her glass, 'if I took you back to mine now, it's safe to say it wouldn't be for some dinner date or a cuddle sesh?'

Maddy blinked. 'Fucking hell. I've only just sat down.'

Chloe look down at the table and smiled, biting her lip. Maddy wanted to roll her eyes. That was some seriously practiced shit, but damn if it wasn't working on her.

'But would you? If I asked?'

'Go back to yours?' Maddy asked.

'Yeah, or we can, you know, sit here making shitty small talk for another hour.'

Maddy considered it, nerves pooling in her belly. Well, that was what she was here for wasn't it?

'Yeah,' she said. 'I would.'

෴

Maddy hadn't considered housemates. It was awkward as hell taking the stairs behind Chloe with the rest of them smirking knowingly from the sofa. But, her mind was made up now and they'd barely taken a step into Chloe's bedroom before Maddy grasped her hip and kissed her.

Chloe's breath stuttered and she let herself fall back against the door, closing it with a click.

'Well, you're not messing around,' Chloe said, pulling back and shedding her jacket.

'Thought we weren't here for a cuddle sesh?'

'We're fucking not.'

Chloe pulled her back in, arms circling fully around her waist. She wasn't a bad kisser, in fact she was really bloody good. Her lips were firm and silky with just the right amount of moisture to them. Maddy would have stopped them then and there if she'd been the slobbery type.

They edged towards the bed. Maddy was down to her bra now and she braced a hand on Chloe's arm as Chloe unclasped the studded belt at her hips.

As her jeans were pulled down, Maddy drew in a steadying breath. Fuck, she was nervous, and way too sober.

'You know,' Chloe said, straightening back up, 'you emo girls are hot and all but getting your skinny jeans off is a fucking nightmare.'

'Worth it though.'

Chloe smiled. 'Go get on the bed.'

In nothing but her underwear, Maddy did as bade. It was chilly in the room and her body goosebumped until Chloe straddled her and slowly began removing her own clothing. Okay, that was kind of hot. Maddy reached out and pressed a hand to the girl's abs, the muscles taught and defined beneath her palm. She followed a line downwards and helped Chloe remove her boxers.

When they were both naked and had been doing nothing but kissing for a while, Maddy became stuck. What did she do now? Was Chloe waiting for *her* to go further or…?

But no, Chloe was shifting now, her hands moving downwards, her head too. When her lips reached her torso, she looked up and asked, 'Can I use my mouth?'

Maddy nodded helplessly. The girl's eyes disappeared and Maddy bit her lip. Shit, this was really happening.

At the first touch, Maddy let out a breath, a slightly louder one for Chloe's benefit. She stared at the ceiling, getting used to the new sensation. It was nice, what she was doing, but there was no way, *no way*, Maddy would get off on it unless the girl had a turbo setting or something.

Her hair was tickly against her thighs and that felt good so she closed her eyes. But when Cerulean's face popped unbidden into her mind, she opened them again and kept them open until she had come. Well, pretended to. God, why was she doing this again?

After she'd gotten the girl off with her hands (had she pretended too or had Maddy actually done a decent job?), they went downstairs and awkwardly drank a cup of tea sat squashed between her housemates.

They were watching some game show and kept stealing glances back at the two of them. Maddy prayed silently for death. She just wanted to go home.

❧ ❦

When Maddy arrived back later that evening, Elise and her parents were sitting in the living room watching TV. Maddy stifled a sigh as she shut the front door—she'd hoped to have made a secret entry. Upon spotting her, Elise put the empty plate from her lap onto the arm of the sofa and pinned her with her attention.

'Where have you been?' she asked, a gleeful accusation in her voice.

'Out,' Maddy replied, savagely shaking her foot to dislodge her boot.

'Out with a *giiirl?*'

Without taking his eyes from the TV, their dad tutted, 'Elise.'

Kicking her boots to the wall, Maddy rolled her eyes and started up the stairs. Fucking homophobe.

In her room, she blew out a loud breath and threw her bag onto the floor before sitting beside it and pulling out her phone. As she fished around for the charging cable, she heard Elise coming up the stairs.

'Oi.'

Without looking up, Maddy replied, 'What?'

'I wonder how they'd feel knowing both of us were dating girls.'

Maddy huffed. 'Yeah.'

'So, who'd you meet then? Someone from that dating site? Phil told me you were speaking to someone.'

'Dick. It's none of his business.'

'Be nice. How'd it go? You've been out for a while.'

Maddy felt heat come into her cheeks. Without meeting Elise's eyes, she said, 'Yeah, I…we went back to hers.'

Elise gave a faux gasp. 'Maddy! On the first date too.'

Maddy shrugged. 'Just lesbians being lesbians. Probably gonna be living together next week, y'know.'

Elise dropped her eyes to the carpet, toeing a patch where Maddy had once singed with her hair straighteners. 'I'm nervous about…you know, with Cerulean.'

'You've only been on one date.'

Elise laughed. 'Says you!'

'Yeah well, I'm the one who makes the bad decisions in this twinship.'

'Are you gonna see her again?'

'Maybe,' Maddy lied.

'What's her name?'

'Chloe.'

'Nice and normal.' Elise leaned back against the doorframe, arms folded. '*Sooo*, do you have any tips for me?'

'Oh my god, I am not having this conversation with my sister. Get out.'

Maddy herded Elise out of her room and firmly shut the door. Finally alone, she took off her jeans, crawled onto her bed and booted up her laptop. But when it came to typing in her password, Maddy stared at the screen, mind zoning out.

So she'd finally had sex with a girl. And it wasn't too bad.

Well, it wasn't great either but it was still a zillion times better than when she'd had sex with a boy for the first time. It had flowed at least, and there hadn't been any awkward stopping and starting or wondering where to put what. Maddy was pretty sure Chloe had had no idea that she'd just taken her lesbian virginity and she was proud of that.

Coming to, Maddy pounded in her password and stabbed at the enter key with feeling. All in all, she was glad she'd gotten it done with. And she hadn't even thought about Cerulean in hours. At least not until Elise had mentioned her. Mentioned *sleeping* with her no less. Gross. That was so not something she wanted to think about. The thought of Cerulean…

Maddy shook her head. 'Fuck off, Mads,' she whispered to herself.

Navigating to her social media, she opened her messages, deciding to regale Phil with a way-too-detailed account of her afternoon. It would serve him right, the gossip. And it would help her to focus on her own sort-of love life instead of that of her bloody sister's.

CHAPTER 19

In the second week of December, Elise shrugged on her winter coat and boots and shouted into the house, 'I'm going! Back later.'

She heard Maddy shout back, 'Where you going?'

'Christmas market. With Cerulean.'

'What?' Elise heard the pattering of feet and then Maddy was in the hallway with her, a vexed look her face. 'But we always do the Christmas market.'

Elise smiled. 'We still can. Next week or something—promise. Or you can maybe go with Chloe.'

Without another word, Maddy stalked away.

When Elise stepped outside, she let out a breath, watching it whirl in the air in one white stream. She was nervous, as per, but the nerves felt different this time, more anticipatory. She'd done nothing but think about Cerulean since their date in the Peaks the other week and it had made a welcome distraction from the normal humdrum of her life.

She still couldn't figure it out—the drying trick. She'd gone over it in her mind, she'd googled it, she'd doubted it had ever happened at all before admonishing herself for gaslighting her own memories. It had bloody happened and today she was going to ask about it.

The most logical thing her brain had come up with was that Cerulean had trained with one of those monks, the ones who could elevate their body temperature crazy amounts and dry the wet shirts they were sitting in. Elise had read an article about it once. Cerulean seemed the well-travelled type; it wasn't too far from the realm of possibility. Bit boring though. Elise much preferred the other things she'd thought of but just as quickly discarded. Like Cerulean was from a lost human evolutionary chain where they hadn't quite lost their magical gifts, or that she was some kind of witch who'd honed her abilities pretty damn well.

Ever since it had happened, her mind had oscillated between being overwhelmingly intrigued to mentally shrugging. Her brain had spent almost a lifetime throwing unlikely scenarios her way and nothing seemed overly weird anymore. So what if Cerulean was an alien, she was hot and Elise liked her.

She was so in her own head that even boarding the bus wasn't the apocalypse and soon she was back in the city, heading towards the markets.

It was late afternoon and the pavement beneath her boots, wet from earlier rains, reflected the Christmas lights strung up everywhere. Elise took a breath, feeling super content all of a sudden. She couldn't wait to see Cerulean, to be taken into those solid arms and kissed. Apart from figuring out Cerulean's magic trick, kissing her again had been something else that was at the forefront of her mind.

The market was packed, as she expected it to be. The undulating crowd made her a bit dizzy but she pushed through, eyes flickering for a glimpse of Cerulean. She found her next to a drinks stall, two steaming cups in her hands. Her face broke into a smile upon spotting her and *god* that smile did things to Elise.

Cerulean pushed off from the stall end and presented one of the cups to her.

'One for the lady,' she said.

Elise took it, inhaling the vapours of the richly mulled wine. 'Thank you.' She peered up at Cerulean, hoping she would take the hint.

Smile deepening, Cerulean grasped Elise's chin and gently kissed her. 'It's lovely to see you again. It has been too long. I feared—well, you kept deflecting my asking to see you.'

'I know.' Elise dropped her eyes to the deep red liquid in her cup. 'I was…thinking.'

'About?'

They began to walk. The crowd disappeared to the back of Elise's mind as her heart began beating double-time. This was a weird place to having this conversation. She'd rather put some food in her stomach first. She was starving and knew the wine would hit her immediately.

'The thing you did,' she said pointedly. 'When I fell into that puddle and then you dried me, somehow.'

'Ah.'

'Gonna tell me how you did it?'

Cerulean inclined her head. 'I could tell you but I'm afraid of the jar of worms it would open. Basilisks, more like.'

Elise looked around. 'Let's get some food. How about churros?'

'Ch-what?'

'Churros! You'll love them, promise—if you have a sweet tooth.'

'That I do.'

When they joined the back of the small queue, Elise shrugged her bag from her shoulder. 'I'll pay,' she said.

But Cerulean put a hand on her arm. 'No, I.'

Elise smiled her thanks, her chest doing some weird swoon at the gallantry. She could put her feminism away for one night. Besides, Cerulean was a girl too so maybe those rules didn't exist here.

Waiting in line, they hastily drank their wines so they had free hands to receive their churros and pots of chocolate sauce. Elise grimaced. Red wine was always so vinegary. Christmas was the only time she'd drink the stuff, and only then if it was hot and spiced.

As expected, the wine quickly flooded her with warmth. As Cerulean paid, she rested her head against the top of

Cerulean's arm, her head tingling as Cerulean's free hand came up to play with her hair.

Cerulean leaned in and said into her ear, 'Smells delicious.'

Elise nodded mutely. She took her food from the vendor and they wandered away to find somewhere less crowded to eat—and talk.

After a couple of minutes walking like that, Elise spotted an unoccupied bench and steered Cerulean towards it. They sat down, churros on their laps. Elise angled her legs so her knees were grazing Cerulean. It was new, this urge to touch and be touched. Until now, Elise had always admired from afar and she was well acquainted with unrequited love as a concept. It felt almost illegal being able to express her attraction like this and it was slightly overwhelming.

They ate their food in silence, watching the Christmas shoppers weaving around them, clutching stall-bought food and drinks. Somewhere, a band was playing and Elise could hear the crackling of a firepit in one of the bars.

Cerulean finished her food first. She gave a satisfied '*mm*', balled up her wrapper and placed the pot of melted chocolate on the bench beside her.

'Good?' Elise asked around a mouthful.

Cerulean nodded. 'Very.' She wrapped an arm around Elise's back. 'Thank you for the introduction.'

'You're welcome.' Elise finished up her own food, feeling a bit buzzed from all the sugar and the wine. She was more than ready to find out what kind of magical sect Cerulean hailed from. 'So.'

'So,' Cerulean repeated.

'Tell me. Who are you, where do you come from and am I the chosen one for your next ritual sacrifice?'

Cerulean tipped her head back, a laugh bubbling up. 'The imagination on you!'

Elise smiled. 'Am I close?'

Cerulean tilted her head. 'I wouldn't say *close*.'

Elise nudged her. 'Tell me. I'll believe you, whatever you

say.'

'Will you?'

'Sure. I'll believe in anything. Aliens, multiverses, Atlantis...'

Cerulean drew in a breath. 'I'm not quite that exotic. I come from a place far away—' Cerulean stopped, putting a hand over her face. 'Heavens, I hated that.'

Elise laughed. 'What?'

Cerulean removed her hand and blew out a raspberry. 'Elise. I cannot. Not like that. Not like this.' She turned to face Elise, picked up one of her hands and kissed a finger. 'I don't wish to sacrifice you.'

'Good to know.'

'But I cannot tell you all in this instance, in this moment. Will you grant me time? Just time.'

Elise nodded. Time was something she could do. Time meant Cerulean would be sticking around. 'As long as you're not planning on killing me, and you're not a fugitive or something, I'll happily carry on with the suspense for a little while longer.'

Cerulean was quiet for a moment, studying Elise. She opened her mouth, closed it again, before finally saying. 'You...are truly a puzzle.'

Elise snorted quietly. 'I'm a puzzle to myself.' She waved a hand in the air. 'Sorry, that was angsty. Just answer me one thing.' Cerulean inclined her head. 'Can you do more? More than just the drying thing?'

When Cerulean smiled, it was dazzling. 'Yes, moon eyes. Much more.'

&∾ ∾&

Elise stepped onto the plush carpet of Cerulean's hotel room, hands clasped in front of her and wringing against the nerves in her stomach.

'Woah,' she said, walking over to the huge windows. 'This is *swaaanky.*'

Behind her, Cerulean chuckled. 'So I'm told.'

'I didn't picture you staying in a place like this.'

'And where had you imagined me?'

'I dunno. You…you dress kind of peasanty.' Elise held up a hand. 'Like, in a good way. I love your style, it really suits you. I just thought you'd be staying in, like, a little cottage or something.'

Cerulean smiled. She was squatting by the open minifridge, eyeing its contents. 'Maybe you and I can go and stay in a little cottage.'

Elise leaned against the window, hands behind her back. 'Maybe. Bet there's some cute ones out in the Peaks.'

Cerulean rose with a pear in her hand. 'Surely you can take that thing off now.'

'What thing?'

Cerulean took a bite of the fruit and pointed at her with it. 'That.'

Elise smiled. 'What have you got against this coat?' In truth, she was warming rapidly, between the heat of the room and the rapid rate of her heart. She felt a bit like a trapped animal. It occurred to her that she'd never been with Cerulean like this, alone in a room. Slowly, she unbuttoned her coat and dropped it to the floor, raising her eyebrows for judgement.

Cerulean looked her up and down. 'Much better.'

A twinge hit Elise in the place between her legs. She pressed further back against the window, feeling pleased about the denim dress she was wearing, the mustard coloured tights like a second skin on her legs.

Cerulean plucked her coat from the floor and tossed it over a chair. Elise half-turned back to the window. The sky was fully dark now but the streets below were lit with Christmas lights, car lights and streetlamps.

Elise's eyes followed the throngs of people who were still out enjoying the Christmas markets. Her brain had checked out big time. Nothing down there looked real. Even the glass felt kind of dubious, like a single push would have her breaking through and plummeting onto the pavement below.

'You are reminiscent of a wood nymph.'

Elise saw a group of men break out into raucous laughter as they left one of the bars but her ears heard nothing but the hum of heating, and the faint sound of Cerulean's voice. 'Hm?'

'The way you stand there so still. Won't you come sit beside me?'

Elise dragged her eyes away from the window. Cerulean was lounging on the bed, nibbling the remainders of her pear from its stem. Elise walked over, stood up one of the pillows and settled against it.

Cerulean held out the pear stem.

'There's nothing left,' Elise said.

'Just a bite. I want to taste it on your lips.'

Oh. Heart racing anew, Elise cupped Cerulean's hand and bought the stem to her mouth, biting off as much as she could, which wasn't much. She'd never been much of a fan of pears anyway. They were too grainy, too mild in taste.

She didn't care about that anymore, not as Cerulean leaned over her and pressed their lips together. In fact, pears had never tasted so good. She'd never felt the weight of another person before, not like this. She couldn't tell if it was more comforting or arousing. Cerulean had flinged the pear stem away and her hand moved to hold Elise's face, fingers threading up through her hair.

When Elise felt a tongue against hers, she froze for just a second before tentatively reaching out with her own. Shit—she was French kissing a girl. She wanted to laugh. She brought her hands up to Cerulean's shoulders and pushed down on them.

Cerulean was practically fully on top of her now. Elise moved one of her legs, slipping it out from under Cerulean and bending it at the knee. It caused Cerulean's thigh to press against just the right place and she clenched her stomach against the urge to push up against it.

Cerulean's lips moved to her neck and Elise didn't think twice about arching her back. Oh, wow. She was sensitive there. She cupped a palm around the curls of Cerulean's head. Cerulean returned to her lips, nipping the bottom one with her teeth, before moving to the other side of her neck.

'You smell heavenly,' she said, nudging the spot behind her ear where Elise had dabbed perfume on earlier. 'Like sugared almonds.'

'Vanilla,' Elise whispered, surprised at how husky her voice was.

'Vanilla,' Cerulean agreed, biting down on her earlobe.

Elise had forgotten about the hand resting on her waist. It moved up now, grazing one of her breasts, before stopping at the buttons to her dress. When Cerulean flicked open the first one, Elise held out a hand to stop her.

'Hang on,' Elise said. Cerulean raised her head and Elise loved how dark her eyes had become. 'Sorry but can we maybe please wait? I know that's boring but, you know, third date rule and everything.'

'You wish to wait?'

Elise nodded slowly. Clearly that wasn't a concept Cerulean was used to. It would be so easy to give in, to give Cerulean what she wanted, what *she* wanted, but she just couldn't so soon. Not on her first time. She didn't want to get to forty and regret having given it up so quickly. Sometimes Elise hated forever living in the future.

'It's my first time,' she explained.

Cerulean searched her eyes. 'You've never…?'

Elise shook her head.

'Okay.' Cerulean licked her lips. 'Okay. I want you Elise, most desperately, but I asked you for time so I can kindly gift some back to you.'

'Thanks,' Elise whispered, feeling both stupid and proud of herself. She reached up and pecked Cerulean on the lips. 'We can keep kissing though.'

Cerulean smiled, already closing the distance. 'I don't think I could stop myself.'

After more heated minutes of doing just that, Cerulean finally pulled away and buried her face in Elise's neck with a frustrated groan.

'Sorry,' Elise laughed, cupping her head. 'We'll stop now. Let's put the telly on or something and just chill.'

She should probably think about going home, but that was the last thing she wanted to do.

With obvious effort, Cerulean disentangled herself and stood up. She found the remote and passed it to Elise before wandering over to the bathroom.

Elise turned on the telly, flicking through the channels until she found some cookery competition then settled into the pillows, waiting for Cerulean's return.

She was gone for a while. Elise glanced at the bathroom door, wondering if Cerulean was maybe… The thought caused her face to flush. She probably shouldn't be thinking of that but then again, they had just been about to have sex.

When Cerulean finally returned, Elise felt too shy to search her eyes for signs that she'd just sorted herself out with a mere door between them.

When Elise finally did look up, Cerulean was smiling at her mildly.

'Slip under the duvet if you want, icy one.'

Elise smiled weakly and pulled back the covers. At the foot of the bed, Cerulean dragged off her trousers, the long tail of her shirt covering anything sinful. God, her legs were so powerful. Her thighs practically bulged and her feet— Elise dug the heels of her hands into her eyes and shook her head. She'd never thought about someone's feet before and she certainly wasn't going to start now.

The bed dipped as Cerulean joined her. They were practically lying side by side and the intimacy of it felt so special to Elise. When Cerulean lifted one of her arms, one brow raised, Elise wasted no time snuggling up to her side, head pillowed on one thick shoulder.

'This is nice,' she said.

Cerulean dropped a kiss to her head. 'I agree.'

They watched the show in comfortable silence before Elise heard Cerulean murmur, 'Fascinating.'

'What?'

Cerulean waved the remote, encompassing the telly.

'The programme?'

'The screen we watch it on. The force which feeds it.'

Elise peered up at her. 'You mean electricity?'

'Electricity,' Cerulean said, smiling. 'I know a girl named Tricity, back home. It makes me wonder if this force was named for her. She has always been fond of this realm.'

'Cerulean, where is home?'

'Below.'

'Below?' Elise frowned. 'Please don't tell me you're some sort of shapeshifting demon. And if you are, please never show me what you really look like.'

'You don't wish to see my true form?'

'Not if you're all, you know, red and—*hellish*.'

Cerulean laughed. 'I am no such thing. Quite the opposite, if you must know.'

Elise raised herself to her elbow, her hair cascading over Cerulean's cheek. She pushed it back over her shoulder. 'This is the weirdest conversation I've ever had.'

Cerulean looked contrite. 'Then we shall halt it.' She nodded at the telly. 'Here—the one in that gaudy dress will win.'

Elise flopped back down. 'How do you know?'

'I have a knack for knowing.'

'One of your powers?'

Cerulean chuckled. 'Quite.'

The gaudy woman did indeed win. Afterwards, Cerulean changed the channel to some farming show. It was insanely boring and Elise felt her eyelids drooping, aided no doubt by the hand on her head which never stopped its stroking.

'Can I stay here tonight?' she murmured.

'I was hoping you would.'

Elise snuggled in further. 'Cool.'

Elise always drifted off easily; the end of the day meant

crashing from the adrenaline perpetually running through her system, and she'd had a lot of it today—the bus, the nerves from seeing Cerulean, the crowds of the market and then the hit of arousal when she and Cerulean had almost had sex. It all made for a goodnight's sleep.

When she woke next, it was to the sound of her phone buzzing on the nightstand. Elise reached out for it, careful not to jostle the arm laying heavy around her waist. They'd changed positions so that Cerulean was now spooning her and oh my god, that felt nice.

Elise squinted as the light from her phone screen assaulted her eyes. She had four texts, all of them from Maddy.

Maddy: When are you back?

Maddy: ??????

Maddy: Hellooo, are you alive???

Maddy: Dude, even Mum's worried. Text meeeeeee

Elise snorted. Absolute drama queen.

Hastily, she messaged back, *Yes, I'm alive, chill. I just fell asleep. I'm staying with Cerulean, back tomorrow xx*

She checked the time—1am. Maybe she should have messaged but she couldn't bring herself to feel bad about it. She put her phone down and wriggled back into the firm warmth behind her.

CHAPTER 20

Maddy reread her sister's text, an acidic churning starting up in her stomach. She hated that this still bothered her, hated it so, so much, but it was beyond her capabilities to stop caring at this point. She blew out a breath through her nose, fingers tight around her phone.

It was in the middle of the night and everything was quiet and still and Maddy couldn't bear it. She needed to be— doing something. Her foot started up a jiggle as she ran through options in her mind. She could just go for a walk but that sounded boring. Phil would no doubt be asleep. Besides, he was sick of her bleating on about Cerulean so that ruled him out. She thought about Chloe. It was Saturday night, she was bound to be out in Manchester somewhere. After their 'date', they hadn't really talked much beyond *hey, did you get home alright?* but Maddy thought that was fine since it was a no strings attached kind of thing.

Without thinking too much, she pulled up their messages and typed, *yo, you out tonight?*

She got a reply back surprisingly quickly: *yeah, I'm at a pal's! We're just about to head out. Why? Are you?*

Maddy replied, *Thinking about it. I'll have to play catch up though. Where you going?*

Chloe: The others want to go to G-A-Y. Meet us there if you want :)

Maddy sat up, flicking on her lamp. She got dressed quickly, pulling on her tightest jeans and a cropped, ripped tank top. From her cupboard, she pulled out some chunky boots and put them on too. She grabbed a can of cider from the fridge and left the house quietly, only calling a taxi once she was safely on the street outside.

The churning abated a bit during the drive. She tried not to think about the fact that she was hurtling towards the city where Elise and Cerulean were—together—and concentrated on downing her cider instead.

The taxi dropped her off near Canal Street and Maddy walked slowly through the throng of drunks, texting Chloe.

Maddy: I'm here

Chloe: We're inside, just at the bar

There was a queue outside the club. While she waited, Maddy pulled out her purse to make sure she actually had her new ID on her because it would suck if she had left it.

Once inside, she pushed through the crowd to the bar, the beat of the music pulsing through her. She couldn't see Chloe, it was way too packed, so she decided to get herself a drink before returning to her search. She ordered herself a double rum. She'd never ordered one before and probably wouldn't again. Too many options. White, dark, spiced? She didn't care, as long as it was a double.

She eventually found Chloe with a group of people on the dance floor close to the bar. Chloe smiled when she spotted her and walked over.

'Hey!' She thrust a cup at her. 'I got you a drink as well.'

Maddy took it in her other hand. 'What is it?'

Chloe grinned. 'Alcohol.'

Maddy smiled. Good enough. After a rushed introduction to her group of friends, Maddy made quick work on the two drinks and the knot inside her finally loosened enough that she was able to enjoy her first proper night out.

And Chloe seemed pretty interested in her too. She hadn't banked on that which was pretty dumb in retrospect. It was nice, dancing with her and sharing little smiles and touches. Her friends seemed to like it too, making kissing gestures whenever Chloe put her hands on her hips as they danced.

Maddy gave herself over to it. She closed her eyes and lifted her face to the purple strobes, feeling so fucking glad that she'd come out.

ॐ ॐ

The moon had moved in the hours that Cerulean had fallen asleep with the human in her arms. It peeked between the buildings in front of hers, flooding the room with its milky white glow. She knew in another thirty minutes, the glow would disappear, hidden again by the concrete towers crowding this city.

She lay on her back, one arm trapped beneath Elise slumbering beside her. Her body still thrummed with the arousal the human had conjured up with her sweet lips and hesitant touches. She wasn't used to it—the denial, the patience. It wasn't in her nature, nor the nature of any of her kind. She would wait though. She'd thrown herself to the mercy of this realm, of its people, of this humanling in particular.

Cerulean turned her head and pressed her lips to a bare shoulder. The skin was cold. Always so damn cold. Cerulean smiled, relishing the sound of pulsing blood which reassured her that, yes, this icy human was in fact alive.

Just as she pressed another kiss to the cold skin, warming it with her magic, her phone bleeped from somewhere in the room. She swivelled her head around before realising it was coming from the floor beside the bed. Gently extracting her arm, she rolled over and plucked it from the carpet. She looked at the screen. Her sister again.

'Risarial.'

'*Wrooong,*' came a sing-song voice through the phone.

'Earlie.' Cerulean cleared the sleep from her voice. 'What?'

'Hello, sister. You have one guess as to where I am.'

'And if I don't guess right?'

Earlie hummed. 'Then I shall feed you to Father's dragon.'

'He doesn't have a dragon.'

Earlie laughed. 'Are you so sure?'

Cerulean glanced at Elise. The girl was awake now, though pretending she wasn't. Cerulean could sense her alertness, the way she listened. 'Where are you then?'

'My mortal's sweet city!'

Cerulean frowned, looking away from Elise. 'You're here? Why?'

'I snuck out.'

'You're an heiress, you don't need to sneak anywhere.'

Earlie tutted. 'Let an heiress have her fun. The guards who are probably just now coming around from their spontaneous sleep would disagree. Now, will you meet with me or not?'

'Not,' Cerulean said slowly.

'Wrong answer.' A pause. 'Cerulean, I fear I am lost.'

Cerulean rolled her eyes. She was always playing these games. Usually Cerulean pandered to her youngest sister but tonight—she was just so comfortable, dammit.

'Where are you?'

Earlie hummed again. 'I cannot be sure but…there's an almighty beast stretched out above me.'

'A beast?'

'All white light. Unmoving but I do not trust it.'

Cerulean sighed. 'An angel. They're called angels. The streets are full of them—they're lights. It's a festival for them soon.'

'Oh, how fun! You must tell me more. Now, right now.'

Cerulean closed her eyes in defeat. 'Fine. Stay where you are. I'll…I'll find you.'

Cerulean hung up. She twisted her head to look at Elise again, stretching her arms out above her as she yawned.

'Moon eyes?'

Elise rolled over. Cerulean smiled, leaning over to kiss

112

her lips. When she pulled back, Elise's eyes were closed again and they would not open until Cerulean returned.

'Sweet dreams for you,' Cerulean whispered.

With one last kiss, Cerulean rolled out of bed and donned her clothes.

ॐ ॐ

By three o'clock, Maddy was pretty drunk. They got bored of the first club and decided to find some food before going somewhere else. Maddy walked alongside Chloe who hadn't moved much from her side all night, despite the various girls who'd approached her.

Maddy was kind of envious. She knew she'd never have what Chloe had, that kind of gay confidence, that subtle androgyny that girls seemed to flock to. Not for the first time, Maddy found herself resenting just how young she looked. It was fine for Elise, she had that good girl, sweet thing going for her. Maddy just looked like a kid trying to look older.

They piled into the nearest place that sold chips and spread out on the red plastic chairs. Chloe pulled Maddy onto her lap, arms loose around her hips.

'Good night?' Chloe asked.

'Not bad.' She put a hand to Chloe's shoulder. 'Stop jiggling your legs. You're gonna make me puke.'

Chloe chuckled. 'Sorry. Fuck, I'm starving.'

Maddy nodded. 'Same.'

'I'm glad you came out.' This was said casually, with no hint of affection. Maddy had found herself looking for that all night, dreading it almost, but Chloe remained nicely chill and aloof.

'Same,' Maddy said again.

When the man behind the counter placed down their Styrofoam containers, Chloe cheered and pushed Maddy from her lap.

'One for you,' she said, passing one to Maddy.

They went back outside and walked aimlessly while they ate.

'Did you fancy anyone tonight?' Chloe asked, shoving four chips into her mouth at once. They were the skinny kind, the ones Maddy loved.

Maddy snorted. 'Fancy?' Shit, it had been years since she'd heard that term.

'Yeah. Plenty of girls were looking at you.'

Maddy glanced at Chloe, disbelief all over her face. 'They were?'

Chloe nodded. 'Yeah but I guess you only had eyes for me.'

Maddy shoved her. 'Get lost. You could have said something. Then I wouldn't have had to kiss you all night.'

Chloe clutched her chest. '*Ouch.* But seriously, is there anyone you're into? And no, I'm not fishing.'

'Then why are you asking?'

'Personal experience.' Chloe shrugged. 'I was just wondering if you were like me, that's all. 'Cause there's this girl. My ex. Well, kind of ex.' Chloe rolled her eyes. 'Because of course there's always 'an ex' when you're a lesbian. Anyway, I love her. Like really fucking, would-do-anything, die-for-her love her. Katie.'

A boy ahead of them whipped his head round to face them. 'Oh my god Chloe! Don't start fucking talking about her.'

Chloe laughed but Maddy saw the pain in her face. She peered closer. Shit, had it been there this whole time? Even when they'd met that first time, when they'd slept together.

'So yeah,' Chloe went on, meeting her eyes. 'Are you? In love with someone else?'

Maddy looked away. 'Can I not just like sex with total strangers?'

'I mean, you *could* but in my experience, girls aren't so good at that. Actually, they're really fucking shit at it.'

Maddy prodded at her chips, suddenly not hungry at all. She wasn't sure she liked this turn of conversation and kind of wished Chloe hadn't opened her mouth at all. She didn't want to know about her shit, not when it ran so parallel to hers. Not that Maddy loved Cerulean. God, she absolutely did not. But it was something just as strong, but way more horrible. Like, way, way more horrible. Maddy didn't even have a word for it.

'I'm not in love with anyone,' she said, but then she looked up, and her eyes latched onto the object of her obsession. She stopped dead in her tracks. Was she hallucinating? She screwed her eyes shut then opened them again. Nope, Cerulean was still there, walking towards her with a blonde girl hooked around her arm. Maddy assumed it was Elise at first but she quickly saw that it wasn't. This girl was taller, more lithe, and absolutely bloody stunning.

When Cerulean met her eyes, Maddy panicked. She started walking again but her legs felt like led, like they wanted to walk in any direction other than this one.

Cerulean smiled. 'Maddy!'

'Where the fuck is my sister?' Maddy blurted, probably a bit too loudly.

The blonde girl turned her face up to Cerulean, a smile of her own on her lips and Maddy hated her, hated her guts, because why the hell was she draped all over Cerulean when Cerulean was supposed to be dating her *sister*?

'In my hotel,' Cerulean said. 'In my bed.'

'Then why aren't you with her? And who's this?'

Cerulean patted the pale hand hooked around her arm. 'This is my sister, Earlie. Earlie, this is Maddy, my—my—the sister of my—'

'Your *girlfriend's* sister,' Earlie, supplied, her face so gleeful that Maddy wanted to slap it.

Cerulean nodded. 'Her *twin* sister.'

'Twins!' Earlie clapped.

Maddy eyed her for a further moment before looking back at Cerulean and snorting. 'Yeah, right. Again, where the hell is Elise?'

'Maddy.' Cerulean reached out and put a hand on her

115

arm. Maddy stiffened. She wanted to jump back but she couldn't because Cerulean was touching her and it was so warm and Maddy hated herself. 'I promise you, she is fast sleep in my room. My sister here needed my assistance. I'm heading back there now. You don't need to worry.'

'I'm not worried,' Maddy lied.

As soon as Cerulean and her *sister* had turned a corner, out of sight, Maddy pulled out her phone and dialled Elise's number.

'Pick up, dick,' she whispered. She swore to god, if Cerulean had murdered her sister, she would fucking—

The phone went to voicemail. Maddy sighed and ended the call, bringing up her messages instead.

'Dude.' Chloe sidled up to her. 'What the hell just happened? Who was that?'

'That was my sister's girlfriend.'

Chloe eyed the direction they went, then turned back to Maddy with something knowing in her eyes. 'She's fit.'

Maddy nodded absently which made Chloe break out in a grin and sling her arm around Maddy's shoulders. 'Mate, do you have the hots for your sister's girlfriend?'

Maddy pushed her away. 'Fuck off.'

Chloe only laughed. 'Oh my god. And I thought my situation was tragic. Anyway, do you wanna stay at mine tonight?'

Maddy nodded. What she really wanted though, was for Elise to wake up and bloody reply to her. She eyed the container of chips she'd thrown to the ground in her haste. This was all so seriously messed up.

❧ ❦

Cerulean leant against one of the bed posts, arms crossed, watching Earlie sitting beside the still slumbering human. There was a lock of Elise's hair between Earlie's finger and thumb, a shade or two darker than her own.

'Pretty,' Earlie said. She drew a fingertip over one of

Elise's eyebrows. Cerulean nodded. 'What is it about her that enraptures you so?'

Cerulean pursed her lips. It was something she was still figuring out herself.

'She wears so many layers. Of clothes. It is cold here, yes, but her mind—it's the same too.' Cerulean shook her head. She was struggling to make sense. 'There are layers there. So many of them, so many it's impossible to know what's at the core and I have to—I must—Earlie, just look at her shoulders!'

At that, Earlie grinned. Cerulean tilted her head and indulged her; Earlie didn't want to know about her human's mind—how dull. Physical appeal was much more intriguing to her.

'They are dainty,' Earlie acquiesced.

'They remind me of Risarial's china. Do you remember? She stole a set—teacups and those tiny stupid plates. They had purple flowers on them and for a week they were all we could drink from.'

Earlie turned to look at her. 'Cerulean, you broke that china. You picked up a teacup, and because Risarial loved it, you dropped it onto the floor and it turned to dust.'

Cerulean suppressed a smirk. Oh, she remembered. She remembered the dark rage in Risarial's face, the ugly twist of her lips. She remembered how a servant came tottering forward but Risarial had already dropped to her knees, scooped up the fragments, then thrown them down at Cerulean's feet before storming from the hall. She was fun to provoke. Cerulean was never proud of herself for it but she was always, always entertained.

The incident reminded her of her run in with Elise's twin earlier. They were quite alike, she supposed—Risarial and Maddy, in some ways. Both quick to rage, both favouring dark colours and grizzly expressions. She wanted to dissect that rage later. Did Maddy truly fear that Cerulean would hurt Elise? Cerulean thought not. No, her anger was the jealous kind and though it was ugly, Cerulean felt an irresistible urge to take a hold of that thread and pull and pull—

'I am hoping this human won't break so easily. Okay, Earlie.' Cerulean unfolded her arms and straightened up. 'Time you were gone now.'

CHAPTER 21

It took a while for Elise to come to the next morning. She felt groggy, like she'd been asleep for too long, or like she was hungover. If it was from the tiny cup of mulled wine the evening before, then she was kind of embarrassed. She wasn't so out of it that she didn't know where she was or who she was with, though.

She turned her head and saw that Cerulean was still asleep. She was on her back, one arm thrown over her head. Her lips were pursed slightly and Elise had to fight the urge to purse her own and kiss them.

On instinct, she picked her phone up and checked the time. 9.30am. No wonder it was so light outside. She also had a shit tonne of texts and missed calls from Maddy and she sighed as she opened them.

Elise read the messages, the furrow in her brow deepening and deepening. What the hell? She glanced at Cerulean then back at her texts. Her sister was seriously messed up. Still, she couldn't help reaching over and running her fingers along Cerulean's arm until she roused.

'Cerulean?'

'Mm?' Cerulean caught her eyes and smiled. 'Morning.'

'Hey.' Elise sidled over. 'This is gonna sound weird but I just got all these texts from Maddy—you know, my sister—and she seems to think she saw you last night.'

Cerulean blinked at her. 'At the market?'

'No. After that. Around three this morning—that was

when she sent the message.'

Cerulean closed her eyes. 'I think you'd know if I'd snuck out in the small hours of the morning.'

'Well, yeah, that's what I thought.' Elise glanced at the phone lying limply in her hand and snorted. 'I'm a super light sleeper, I would have known if you'd disappeared on me. She said you were with some other girl…'

'You were the only person I was with last night.'

Elise smiled. 'Promise?'

Instead of answering, Cerulean rolled herself on top of Elise and kissed her soundly. Elise grabbed onto those firm, strong arms and feeling only slightly self-conscious about her morning breath, kissed her back.

Cerulean's lips moved to her neck. 'Does this count as the third date?'

Elise laughed breathlessly. 'I'm not doing it with you now! I slept in my clothes, I feel all sweaty and gross.'

Cerulean inhaled. 'You still smell like heaven to me. Do you not want me?' she teased.

'Of course I want you,' Elise whispered. 'It's just—I've never done this with a girl before.'

'I know. You said.'

'No, I mean—Cerulean, I didn't even know I was into girls before I met you. This is all just very…new.'

Cerulean took her into her arms and Elise lay there with her eyes closed, feeling a bit pathetic. She couldn't help but think of Maddy. Maddy would have given it up by now. She wouldn't be thinking about regret that may or may not surface sometime in the future. She would just do what she wanted to in the moment and probably never question it again. The thought made her feel envious and a bit uncertain. Maybe Cerulean had picked the wrong twin after all.

'Cerulean, can I ask you something?'

'Of course.'

Elise lifted her head. 'Why did you pick me? Over Maddy, I mean. You know she's the gay one, don't you?

120

And she likes you, you know.' Elise didn't know why she was saying these things. They weren't making her feel good. 'You'd only have to say the word and she'd be with you.'

'And what about who I want?'

'Well, that's what I'm asking. Why me and not her? She's way more fun than me. Way more adventurous and—'

'Elise.' Cerulean put a finger on her lips. 'I don't really know how to tell you how I see the both of you but—Maddy is fire and you are air. Maddy favours the dark and you the light.' Cerulean smiled. 'I enjoy the balance but I, myself, favour the light, most of all.'

Elise flopped back down. 'Oh,' she said. 'Okay.' That made sense, kind of. Her and Maddy were complete opposites but it was easy to forget their differences when their faces were identical and Elise was jealous of all the things she could never be, all the things Maddy was, even the things Elise hated the most about her.

Cerulean cleared her throat. 'May I treat you to breakfast? The hall downstairs—it serves the most delectable pastries and tiny thimbles of tea.'

Elise smiled. 'You may.'

☙ ❧

Maddy laid on her stomach, facing away from Chloe in the bed, scowling at the only message she had from Elise this morning: *Stop meddling! xx*

Maddy sighed and rolled onto her back.

'What are you huffing about?' Chloe asked, voice muffled with a yawn.

'Nothing. My stupid sister.'

'Your stupid sister and her hot as fuck girlfriend.'

'Didn't think you went for girls like that.'

'I don't, but *you* do.' Chloe rolled over and faced her, smiling impishly. Her long hair was all over the place and her lips were redder than usual. Maddy couldn't help but look.

'I don't.'

Chloe hummed her disbelief. Beneath the duvet, her hand found its way to Maddy's stomach and stopped there, thumb stroking bare skin. They'd had sex again last night, Maddy suddenly remembered, and she'd actually had an orgasm this time. It wasn't the best one she'd ever had, she'd had to strain for it, but she was glad she could actually get there with someone else touching her. She had begun to overthink it.

'Wanna stay for breaky?' Chloe asked. 'Or is that too intimate for you?'

Maddy grimaced. 'Don't think I could eat right now. Might just head home.'

'That's cool.' Chloe picked up her phone. 'I'll ring you a taxi, since I'm a gentleman.'

Maddy got home before Elise. She was kind of glad about that. She didn't have the stomach for a fight and fighting seemed to be something she was so good at lately.

She tried not to think about the night before, tried not to worry about Elise. There was a stupid voice in her head telling her that Cerulean could have sent that message this morning from Elise's phone and Elise could still be murdered and dead. It was a dumb thought, Maddy knew, but the worry was only slightly better than the anger and jealousy. Only slightly.

In the kitchen, she made herself a sandwich, nodding at her dad who was sat at the table tapping at his tablet. He nodded back and Maddy retreated upstairs with her plate. The thought of eating right now made her want to hurl but she'd save the sandwich for later. That way she could spend the whole day in her room and stay out of everyone's way, especially Elise's.

CHAPTER 22

There were two things Elise thought about these days—the inevitability of losing her virginity and the person she'd be losing it to and that person's—gifts? Abilities?

She wasn't sure which she thought about the most. It would usually start with the memory of them squished together in the crevice of the rock, with Cerulean's fingers dancing over her trousers, wicking the dampness away, which would inevitably lead to flashbacks of their first kiss, and then their second, and so on, until she was thinking about the ins and outs of having sex.

She had a routine in her head, of where she'd touch Cerulean first and how she'd do it. She knew it probably wouldn't go down like that but it eased her anxiety to be somewhat prepared.

She made a promise to herself, though, that she wouldn't let any of that happen until she knew Cerulean's true nature.

She'd never skipped college before but when Cerulean messaged her on her lunch break with a location and a request to meet *now*, she was powerless to say no.

Thankfully she only had English with Maddy that day and that had happened earlier on, so she'd be none the wiser. Elise only had Philosophy left after lunch. It was probably her most difficult subject, and she had exams next month, but she tried not to think about that as she made her way to the bus station.

The location Cerulean had given her was pretty close to

her house, on the road which ran along the edge of the woods. Elise tapped it in on her phone and zoomed in. Lots of green. Not much else. Elise wondered where Cerulean wanted to take her. It made her nervous, the not knowing. Besides, she didn't know Cerulean *that* well... She blew out a breath, fogging up the bus window. Knowing Cerulean was her current mission. She stamped down on her anxiety and held to that.

The bus turned onto the road running alongside the woods and Elise got off at the next stop. She continued along the path as the bus pulled away, darting looks through the shrubbery at her side. The day was overcast and it was dark beneath the trees.

Cerulean was waiting for her beside one of the paths into the woods, leaning against a wooden fence choked in ivy. She pushed off it at the sight of Elise and grinned.

'Hey,' Elise said. Cerulean reached out and cupped her cheeks. God, so warm. Elise closed her eyes as she was kissed. 'Where we going?'

'I've acquired something I think you might like. I want to show you.'

'In the woods?'

Cerulean nodded and started down the path.

'Gonna tell me what?'

Cerulean glanced back at her. 'Don't you allow yourself any surprises?'

'Not if they involve me disappearing off into the woods.'

Noticing her apprehension, Cerulean slowed and took her hand. 'You will really like it,' she said.

'Okay. I'll take your word for it.' Elise looked around. It was an ancient woodland, this one. Or so her parents had told her. They had pointed out old lime trees and told her why the water in the streams was so red and explained the geology of the bedrock. 'God, it's been years since I've been through here,' Elise said. 'We used to go all the time when we were younger, when we first moved here. Me and Maddy were about eight, I think. We loved the woods then.'

'It has charm,' Cerulean said. 'More energy here than in a roomful of your kind.'

Elise looked up through the bare branches above her. 'Not your kind then?'

'No, but I think you're beginning to understand that.'

Elise hummed. 'Not quite. You're the queen of evasion.'

Cerulean regarded her through the dim of the woods. 'Maybe tonight that changes.'

Elise felt the finality of that in her heart, a strange mix of excitement and foreboding. They continued to walk until they came to a fork in the path, which snaked off in three ways. Cerulean looked at the sign posted there then tugged Elise in the direction heading right.

Everything was grey apart from the dark teal of holly shrubs and patches of grass lining the path. The path narrowed for a few turns before widening into something more cultivated.

'Nearly there,' Cerulean said.

In the distance, Elise spotted a wall dotted with bleached lichen, and a wire fence between the dead and twisted bramble bushes.

As they came up to the wall, Elise spotted the vintage sign nailed there which read *Bradcroft Cottage*.

Cerulean slowed down as the house came into view around the wall. 'You were right,' she said. 'This place suits me much better than that glass tower.'

'Woah, you're renting this?'

'It is mine. For now.'

Cerulean stepped up to the door and pushed it open.

'That's so cool! Me and Maddy used to *love* this house. We were convinced it was a witch's cottage. We used to try and find it, with Mum and Dad, and sometimes we couldn't. Got lost or whatever. So we used to think it was magic, only appearing at certain times.'

Cerulean pulled off her boots and smiled. 'How do you know you weren't wrong?'

'*Bleh*. Don't mess with my head.' Elise looked around the

quaint kitchen, with its aga and windowsill herb planter and saucepans hanging from a beam. 'Yeah, this definitely suits you. Can I look around?'

'Be my guest. Let me make us tea. I know that short walk will have frozen your veins.'

With the sound of the teakettle whistling in the background, Elise poked her head round the other rooms in the cottage—a living room, bedroom, bathroom and a tiny utility room. Everything was painted a pale green, like it was part of the forest itself. If it wouldn't give her away, Elise would be telling Maddy all about this.

'This is a cottagecore dream,' Elise said, returning to the kitchen. 'I love the garden. All those animal statues are so cute.'

Using a checkered tea towel, Cerulean grasped the handle of the teakettle and poured into two mugs. 'Glad you approve. I hoped you would.'

They sat down at the tiny table and blew on their teas. It was very quiet. There was no hum of heating or distant voices. No birds or wind. Elise fidgeted, deliberately burning her fingertips on the mug to ground herself. She looked over at Cerulean who looked right back.

'You say so much in just a look,' she said quietly.

'What am I saying?' Elise asked.

'I see many things which all simply boil down to *who are you?*'

'More like *what?*' Elise smiled ruefully. 'Which makes me kinda mad. I think I need you to make me not mad.'

Cerulean rested her head in her palm. 'This is so delicate,' she murmured. 'I am almost…afraid.'

Elise picked up her mug and took a sip. 'Of?'

'The effect. Which is strange. I usually love the effect. The fallout.'

Elise shook her head. 'My mind's derailed already.' She looked over her shoulder. 'Can we go look at the garden? I wanna see that pond at the back.'

Elise grasped her mug firmly between her hands as they

walked back outside. The garden was large and overgrown but Elise reckoned it would be stunning come springtime. They walked past statues of badgers, hedgehogs and mushrooms until they came upon the large pond.

'Manmade,' Cerulean said, disappointed.

Elise took a deep breath. 'Water's water,' she said, and thrust her cup at Cerulean.

She tried to keep her mind blank as she took one step forward, and then another, until she was lurching down the tiny bank and into the pond.

At the first touch of the icy water, her entire body froze, but she kept on going until she was up to her knees. The water continued to darken the fabric of her trousers.

When it touched the tops of her thighs, she finally turned and trudged back onto the lawn, dripping and shivering uncontrollably.

She peered at Cerulean and said, 'Do something then.'

Cerulean dithered for a moment before lowering the mugs to the grass and reaching out for Elise. 'Come here.' She took Elise into an embrace. 'You devious thing,' she whispered.

Elise closed her eyes as the most delicious warmth travelled up her legs. It didn't stop there, continuing on until it enveloped the whole of her. 'God, that's so nice.'

They stood that way for a while as the heat seeped away. Elise leaned back. 'Sorry. Had to check.' She searched the blue of Cerulean's eyes. 'Tell me,' she said. 'You have to. This is driving me mad.'

For a long while, Cerulean stared before a smile began to pull at her lips. 'Let me show you instead. I'm not sure simple words would suffice for the likes of you.'

There was a gleeful light in Cerulean's eyes as she pulled Elise through the garden gate and back into the woods.

Elise's heart was hammering and her mind had long gone bye-bye. They walked into the heart of the woods to an avenue of trees, the other end of it lost in shadow.

Cerulean turned to Elise and Elise tensed at the look in

her face—intense, focused. In her peripherals, she saw Cerulean's hands curl into fists and then light began emanating from her. Her skin lit up in a buttery yellow glow and it bounced off the grey tree trunks around them, lighting up the avenue.

'*Wha..?*' Elise looked her over, not comprehending. 'How are you doing that?'

'I'm not. Not doing, that is. I'm just being.'

'Yeah, but how?' Elise reached out blindly and her hand snagged on a shrub. It was holly but she didn't care. The spikiness was welcome. It made her feel real.

'This is me, Elise.'

Her skin was different. Smoothed over, utterly flawless. Like a filter. Elise yearned to touch it but she was still grasping the holly.

She looked away. She had to. But everything was brighter now, all glowy and soft. She felt part of a painting, some whimsical European fairy tale. There'd be bears padding down the avenue next, and owls departing wisdom from the branches above.

'Elise.'

'Mm?'

'Want to see more?'

Elise nodded and they continued walking. The light seeped away eventually and Cerulean looked like her Cerulean again. Mostly. It was all kind of changed now.

They came to a tree trunk crisscrossed with vines, dead leaves flapping listlessly against it. Cerulean squatted down. There was a smile on her face. Wholly unconscious. Elise wasn't sure what to make of it.

As she watched, Cerulean reached out and cupped her hands around a leaf. Elise knew what was coming next, she just knew. She almost felt nothing as the leaf bloomed green again. Cerulean looked up at her and it was an effort to smile back.

'What else?' Elise whispered, helpless not to.

Cerulean stood to her full height and stepped in close.

128

'Close your eyes,' she whispered, enclosing her arms around Elise.

Elise grasped her arms, feeling entirely unbalanced. She drew in a breath as she felt the ground leave her feet. She couldn't open her eyes now if she wanted to. She knew they were in the air. She'd dreamed of flying before and if she kept her eyes closed, she could pretend it was just that.

When her toes touched the ground again and she finally cracked her eyes open, Cerulean was standing there grinning. 'Fairing okay, moon eyes?'

Elise shook her head. 'I am this close,' she said, pinching her thumb and finger together, 'to losing my mind entirely.'

'Oh dear,' Cerulean murmured. 'Oh no, no. We can't have that.' She leaned forward and took the finger into her mouth, smiling around it.

The wet heat hit Elise straight between the legs. She couldn't look away, eyes riveted on Cerulean's mouth, her finger lost within it. She felt a tongue lick the tip then Cerulean released it with a pop.

'Come back to the cottage?' she asked, voice low.

Elise nodded, feeling the cold swirl around her fingertip, and the weight of what she knew she'd just agreed to. But for once, the familiar anxiety was welcome. It made her feel real, grounded, *human*.

Back at the cottage, Cerulean walked her to the small bedroom, shut the door, then removed her coat and cardigan before telling her to get onto the bed.

Elise did, trying to relax her body and take her mind off the fact that she was minutes away from losing her virginity. She tried to bring to mind her plan, the one she'd gone over and over in the solitude and safety of her own bedroom, but it was hard to think of anything once the weight of Cerulean settled over her.

They kissed for long moments, long enough for Elise to relax and become impossibly warm under Cerulean's heat. She was even hotter now. Elise stroked her palms up and down Cerulean's back, smoothing over the thin shirt she wore.

Elise moved her leg, like she had in the hotel, bending her knee so Cerulean pressed against her in just the right spot. She let out a breath and felt Cerulean respond by pressing kisses to her neck, and her hands began toying with the bottom of her top.

'May I?' Cerulean breathed, fingers slipping beneath to touch the skin of her stomach.

Elise nodded wordlessly and let Cerulean divest her of her top and jeans. She knelt up and did the same to herself but unlike Elise, Cerulean wasn't wearing any underwear. God, she was so strong. Elise felt shy looking but it was easier than looking into her eyes. Her gold skin was roped with muscle, muscle which bunched and released as Cerulean removed Elise's last few layers of clothing.

When one of Cerulean's hands moved downwards, Elise closed her eyes and kept them closed for the rest of the time. She felt less self-conscious that way, free to really feel what Cerulean was doing to her. She reached the end quicker than she thought she would, covering her face with her hands and breathing harshly through her mouth.

Oh my god. She opened her eyes, her vision blurry from having them closed for so long. Cerulean hovered above her and the abject longing on her face made Elise tense up. God, what was she supposed to do again? She didn't have any time to figure it out before Cerulean took one of her hands and pressed it between her legs.

Oh, that was strange. Elise didn't even want to consider the expression on her face as she searched with her fingers, looking for *that* spot. When she thought she had it, she relaxed back into the bed and stared up at Cerulean's face. It was weird, touching someone who wasn't herself. Elise couldn't look away. Cerulean leaned on one elbow, her face a mix of both concentration and pleasure.

It didn't take long. Elise sped up when Cerulean's breaths became more urgent until Cerulean reached down and pressed her fingers against her, stiffened, and let out two low groans so passionate, they almost set Elise off again.

Eventually, Cerulean lifted her head and Elise smiled, pushing damp curls from her forehead. Cerulean's breathing was laboured, mouth slightly parted. Her face was so serious. Elise let out a chuckle, thinking it was strange seeing that mouth do anything but smiling.

'To laugh at a woman after they've made love to you might be the worst offence.'

'Sorry,' Elise whispered. 'I'm not laughing at you, not really.' She licked her lips. 'That was—that was super good.'

Now Cerulean smiled. 'For me, too. You were perfect.'

'I'll get better, promise.'

'I will gladly take any promises from you.'

Cerulean took her hand, the one that had just been touching her, and kissed each one of her fingers. Elise was sure, in that moment, that she loved her.

Afterwards, Cerulean walked her to the alley which ran along the back of her house, but instead of going home, she kissed Cerulean goodbye then made her way to her log in the clearing.

As she had plenty of times, she lit up a cigarette and breathed in its smoke but barely took a drag. Her mind was miles away; she didn't feel like herself and it felt wonderful.

She knew there was still stuff they needed to talk about, a whole lot of it probably. Cerulean had shown her plenty but she hadn't *told* her a thing. That could come later. Elise didn't want to think about it right now. She just wanted to feel.

Just when the cigarette neared the quick, she heard the crunching of leaves and slowly turned her head, watching her sister approach with a frown on her face.

'What are you doing?' Maddy asked.

'How did you know I was here?'

'I saw you when I was getting off the bus. Saw Cerulean walk off. Did you bunk college?'

'Just one lesson.' The cigarette burned out and Elise

131

looked at the blackened tip for a moment before dropping it to the floor.

Maddy raised her arms, encompassing the clearing. 'Why do you do this?'

Elise let out a breath. Her mood was fading. She felt embarrassed and…foolish. Damn Maddy. Thank *god* she hadn't put on the t-shirt buried under the log.

'It's just a thing.'

'But why? You hate smoking. You hate it when I do it.'

Elise stood up. 'Yeah, well.' She stalked past Maddy and out of the clearing.

'It's weird,' Elise heard from behind her. Elise ignored her and unlatched the garden gate. 'Mum's home,' Maddy continued. 'She'll smell the smoke.'

'Mum couldn't give a shit.'

Elise hooked her coat quickly and bounded up the stairs to her bedroom, locking the door and pulling out her headphones. She didn't want to feel normal again so quickly; she blasted her music against the intrusion. If Maddy knocked on her door at any point, she didn't hear it.

CHAPTER 23

Maddy flattened herself against the shop shelves as a staff member squeezed past, outfitted in fishnet tights and pink mesh gloves. She must have been freezing.

The fluorescent lights above her were flickering, bouncing off the box of hair bleach in her hand. She sent them a baleful glare, replacing the bleach back on the shelf.

'So the Chloe thing isn't working?' Phil asked from beside her, fingering a tub of coral hair dye.

'Not really.'

Phil pursed his lips. They were bright magenta today and satiny like he'd just eaten greasy fish and chips. 'Well, someone else then?'

Maddy sighed, plucking a cheaper box of hair bleach and a tub of blue dye. 'No Phil. No one else.'

They walked down the aisle rammed with brightly coloured alternative beauty items. The only other customers in here were college kids like them.

'I think they've had sex. Her and Elise,' Maddy said.

'Probably. They've been together a while now.'

Maddy clamped her jaw against the urge to scream in his face. How did no one get how much this was messing her up? Elise had told her about the cottage in the woods, the one they used to make up stories about. Tainted, now. She hoped to never walk past the damn place again.

'Sure you wanna dye it blue?'

Maddy glanced at the tub in her hand. 'Why not? If I

hate it, I'll dye it out again.'

'You're gonna fuck your hair up.'

'It's already fucked.' She tugged at a strand. It was so dry and teased to hell and back that it just stayed there until she smoothed it back down again. As they walked to the till, she eyed the cubicles where they pierced people. 'I wanna get my bellybutton pierced.'

'What—now? We have to go back in ten.'

'You can go back, I'm getting my belly button pierced. Here, buy this for me. I'll pay you back.' Maddy thrust her items into Phil's hands.

'What? But—dude, come on. Let's go to Photography first. We can come back after.'

Maddy waved him off. 'Nah. I'll see you later.'

She caught the eye of a piercing technician and stalked over to him. Ten minutes later, she'd filled out her little form and was being led into one of the cubicles. It was tiny, only room enough for a bed and a narrow ledge where the piercing equipment was kept.

Maddy laid down and pulled up her top when directed. She eyed the ceiling, waiting for that stab of pain. When it was done, she glanced down. The belly bar was blue, as blue as Cerulean's eyes and Maddy immediately regretted the choice. She'd buy another and change it when she got home and pray nothing got infected.

She didn't go to Photography in the end. She wandered through town and towards a shopping precinct which held furniture and electronics shops. In the corner beside a Starbucks was a large pet shop. Maddy walked towards it, suddenly inspired.

Inside stank of hay and dog kibble. Maddy headed for the pet adoption centre in the middle and pressed her face close to the tanks, trying to spy the tiny rodents. A hamster was clawing at the glass of one of them, its fur long and sticking up in the same way Maddy's hair did in the mornings. She left it scrabbling, hoping it would still be there when she returned.

She needed a cage, and food, and probably other stuff but she could get all that later. For a whole twenty minutes while she compiled everything, she didn't think of Cerulean. She felt a surge of pure triumph as the attendant enclosed the hamster into a box and handed it to her. It was a faff and a half to carry everything out of the shop. She didn't bother with the bus; placing everything down onto the side of the road, she ordered a taxi and headed home.

Thankfully, her parents weren't in and Elise was still at college, so she managed to sequester everything to her room unnoticed. Once she'd assembled the cage and the hamster was safely inside, she turned on her laptop and began researching. She'd need a bigger cage, she knew that, and whatever else to make that hamster the happiest damn hamster in the whole world.

For a full two hours, she didn't think of Cerulean.

CHAPTER 24

Elise sat cross-legged on her bed, a philosophy textbook splayed open on her thighs. The words jumped with the firelight of the three candles she had going on her bedside table. She should probably flick on her lamp but she liked the light like this—all glowy and quiet.

Her A-level exams, the last of them, were next month. She hadn't forgotten—couldn't, with her mum banging on about them. Mostly to Maddy. She assumed Elise would be knees deep in revision by now. Elise snorted. If only she knew. If only she knew Elise couldn't concentrate on a thing because out there, somewhere, was an impossible girl who'd appeared out of nowhere and made a home in every crevice of her mind—and heart.

Elise looked over at the window, where orange jumped over the panes. The sky was pitch black. It was pretty late, though Elise could still hear muffled bass sounding from Maddy's room across the hallway. Her parents were probably still up too, corralled away in the study, compiling their dull reports. They were all night owls in this family.

Elise drew in a breath and bent her knees to her chest, pulling the book closer so she could read better. The page was about some medieval philosopher. It was kind of dry and all a bit…small. Especially now. Did he know? This philosopher—was he aware that there were people who could generate heat at the mere thought of it, could bring dead foliage back to life, could *fly?* Elise doubted it. She hoped he was up in his heaven now, amazed at how much of life he hadn't known.

Elise blew out a raspberry and turned the page. A second later she was peering over at the window again, drawn away from the book by a gentle knocking sound. Elise stared at Cerulean behind the glass for a second too long, only stirring when Cerulean pointed at the window latch, one eyebrow raised, a grin on her face.

'Oh my god,' Elise breathed, tossing the book from her lap. Her heart beat wildly. She was in her pyjamas and her hair was thrown up in a bun, badly needing a wash, and Cerulean was outside her window like some lover of old. She hadn't even texted. Elise felt both elated and off-kilter at once.

She pulled open the latch and gently pushed it open, careful not to whack Cerulean.

'How the hell did you get up here?' Elise whispered, standing back as Cerulean hauled herself over the windowsill.

Her knees hit crystals and tealights, sending them clattering, and she grimaced apologetically. 'Do you really need to ask?'

'You…' Elise considered the height from the front garden to her bedroom. 'You flew?'

Cerulean darted forward and kissed her. 'Right. And I intend to fly right back down. With you.'

Elise tucked some flyaways behind her ear, hoping the low light would hide its state. 'How do you mean?'

Cerulean smiled. 'I was hoping you could visit my home with me.'

'The cottage?'

'No.' Cerulean leaned against the window ledge and folded her arms. Elise folded her arms too; it was freezing with the window open. 'I know I haven't assuaged any of your wonderings, only created more. And as I said before— showing trumps telling so show you I would like.'

'In the middle of the night though?'

'I'll have you back by morning. You have my word.'

Elise hesitated. Nerves clawed at her. It really was pitch black out there, and cold, and Elise had never—'Where is home? How far?'

Cerulean tilted her head. 'It varies. Closer in the dark. A smattering of your hours. Bring that big coat of yours, icy one.'

Elise looked around her room; her cosy, comforting room. 'Will I be safe?' she asked hesitantly. She gave a little laugh. 'Stupid question, I know…'

'Yes.' Cerulean reached out and took her hand. 'My word on that, too.'

Elise drew in a breath. 'Okay. Let me just…I need to change. Five minutes, okay?'

Cerulean nodded and sat down on the bed. Elise walked over to her bedroom door and locked it. Last thing she needed was someone barging in right now. She shut the window too, still shivering, and set about changing into clothes.

'My coat's downstairs,' she said when she was done. 'I'll have to go down and get it and sneak out. Shall I meet you in the garden or do you want to risk it with me?'

Cerulean blew out the candles and stood up. 'Risk it with you.'

'Okay. Quiet, though.'

Elise unlocked her door and stepped out into the corridor where Maddy's music became louder. 'Maddy's room,' she said, waving a hand dismissively at the closed door.

'I know. I remember.'

Of course. Elise recalled the party, where she'd watched the two of them exit from Maddy's room. She felt a pang of…guilt, was it? Maddy had been interested in Cerulean that night, probably still was, even now. Elise took a breath to dispel the sensation. She wasn't doing anything wrong. It was Maddy who was making everything so bloody tense. She wished her sister would get a grip and let it go. She kind of missed hanging out with her and talking about inconsequential stuff. These days, Cerulean was always a massive elephant in any room they found themselves in.

In the kitchen, Elise took her coat from the peg, slipped it on, and rolled open the patio door as quietly as she could. In the alleyway behind the house, Elise paused again. Though she couldn't see it, her clearing with the log was only a few paces away. Elise of the woods would do this. She'd sneak out at any hour of the night, feeling just as comfortable in the dark as she would the day. So would Maddy, but she tried not to think about that.

'Which way do we go?' she asked, her voice quiet against the night.

Her hand was taken. 'This way.'

For a time, they walked along the road, dipping in and out of pools of light from the streetlamps and Elise felt fine. Then Cerulean turned down one of the forest paths and everything became impossibly black. Anxiety clawed at her and she knew her eyes were wide as they tried to penetrate the blackness. A girl was raped in these woods last year, and it had been at an earlier hour than this. Elise tried not to think about that, tried to glean safety from the girl at her side. If Cerulean could bring back dead plant matter, then maybe she could…whatever the opposite of that was.

'I can't see,' she finally said when her foot caught on a root.

'Can't you?'

'Well, can you?'

'Quite clearly.'

'I'm turning on my phone torch.' Elise thrust her hand into her pocket.

'No need,' Cerulean said and then her skin was glowing like a thousand fireflies.

Elise stared. 'You're kinda handy. Super freaky, but handy.'

Cerulean grinned. 'I am fortunate in my gifts. It is never quite full light at home.'

'Are you all born that way? With gifts and stuff?'

'My family, at least. Our bloodline—it's an ancient one. Diluted now over many hundreds of years. Our 'gifts' are merely party tricks now.'

Elise snorted quietly. *Party tricks, wow.* 'So, can your sisters glow and stuff too?'

Cerulean shook her head. 'They cannot. Risarial—she's the oldest—she can emulate the way of trees.' Cerulean whipped out a hand, making Elise jump. 'Can just strangle you with a vine from the palm as quick as you like. It was her favourite way to whip us into shape when we were younger. And Earlie, well, she has a way of making you do whatever you like. She doesn't much need gifts. I'm wise against her wiles of course but the rest of the court—not so much.' Cerulean pursed her lips like she was trying not to smile. In her strange light, they shined like strawberries under the sun.

'I'm nervous,' Elise said, looking away. 'About visiting your home. I'm worried I won't…fit in right.'

'Then worry not.' Cerulean squeezed her hand. 'Humankind isn't as foreign to us as we are to you. Besides, I don't plan on letting you out of my sight.'

That eased Elise's anxiety somewhat.

'Do humans live there?' She felt a bubble of embarrassment asking that. It was so dumb, entertaining all this.

'A small number, yes,' Cerulean said quietly.

Could I? It was right on the tip of her tongue but she bit it back, cheeks flushing. She didn't even know where *there* was. Was she really that desperate for escape?

'Tell me what it looks like,' she said instead. 'Tell me all the things.'

Cerulean chuckled. 'One day you will know a true surprise and you will like it.'

Elise ducked her head and smiled wryly. She listened as Cerulean talked, eyes low on the glowing forest path beneath her feet. A picture formed in her mind—of mist, of

141

dusky skies and damp earth. She could almost smell it. Cerulean was an incredible story weaver, her voice slow and intimate. Elise had the urge to write down everything she was saying before remembering that this was all supposed to be real.

After a while, Cerulean trailed off. Elise glanced at her, noticing her peering through the trees.

'What is it?' Elise looked around too. Cerulean didn't answer—she didn't have to. A moment later, she could hear the music too. It was twinkly and jovial, like flutes and windchimes. 'Cool party,' she commented, hoping silently that it wasn't some weird cult meetup.

Another few steps and she could see lights that didn't belong to Cerulean and the occasional flash of a body as they danced through the trees, upsetting shrubbery.

'What *is* that?' Elise slowed to a stop and her eyes suddenly caught another's. She relaxed when she saw it was only a girl, one about her age, leaning back against a tree. She had bobbed hair, the same colour as Elise's but thicker and slightly wavy. The girl raised her hands and pulled it all back from her face. Elise could see her chest heaving. She looked like she'd just ran a marathon but she managed to flash Elise a small smile before pushing hard off the trunk and disappearing.

'A revel not meant for us,' Cerulean said, tugging on her hand. 'Not tonight.'

Elise shook her head. 'Everything's so weird. Just so weird.'

They walked for a while more until the forest abruptly fell away, opening up onto a dark grassy plain. Elise felt a distinct nothingness ahead of them after the busyness of the forest.

'I believe we are here, just about,' Cerulean announced, looking around with a pleased smile.

Elise frowned. 'We're *here*? Already? You said it would take hours.'

'And hours it has been!'

Elise fished for her phone in her pocket. No way had it been hours. An *hour*, maybe. But no, her phone showed 3am—three hours after they'd left. 'I'm confused,' she said, repocketing her phone.

Cerulean turned so she was walking backwards. 'Time is different where I'm from, and the places between here and there.'

Elise stared. 'Where are you from, Cerulean? You haven't actually said.'

Cerulean pointed downwards. 'Below.' She pursed her lips. 'Or across, depending on your point of passage.'

Elise nodded slowly, reaching out blindly for Cerulean's hand again, needing the anchor. 'And how do we get…*below*?'

'Many ways, most closed to you—or at least, very hidden. See the mist there?' Elise looked where Cerulean was pointing but there was nothing but blackness. She shook her head. 'Well, soon you will. My home lies on the other side of the white.'

Elise toyed with a toggle on her coat, running the cool plastic tip along her lips. 'I'm guessing that's not on any maps.'

'Not yours. Not anymore.'

'So, a different realm then? A super hidden one?' Elise bit her lip, a laugh threatening to bubble up. Cerulean gave a nod. 'And you're…you are—you know—*human,* like me?' Cerulean shook her head, an almost chagrined smile on her lips. 'Then what?'

'Your kind has many names for ours, most of them unfavourable—those of which I quite like.' Cerulean flashed her teeth. 'I think, in these times, you refer to us as fae-kind. A myth, merely, though we remain quite real.'

Elise raised her eyebrows. 'Fairies?'

'If you wish. Though it's more my youngest sister that you'll find tucked up in a flower's bud, befriending all the weevils and Muridae.'

Elise didn't speak for a while after that. She was tilling

over the information Cerulean had just given her, waiting for her brain to catch up. Maybe it was the cold, or the dark, but it was having a hard time of it. She was holding hands with a fairy. Elise stroked her thumb over Cerulean's hand, her only point of warmth. What made it so warm, what made Cerulean—*fae-kind*? How much did they differ? Hopefully not too much. They'd had sex. Elise blinked against the dark. That line of thinking wasn't helping anything. And was she even believing any of this anyway?

She could see the mist now, though. 'Is there water there?'

'Yep. Our way in.'

'God, don't tell me you have gills too.'

Cerulean chuckled. 'Now wouldn't that be a hoot.'

Elise breathed out against the rising nerves in her stomach as they approached the mist. She thought she could hear the gentle lapping of water but wondered if it was just her imagination, her senses kicked into overdrive in the dark.

The earth began to squelch beneath her shoes and she regretted not wearing her boots.

'Careful,' Cerulean said and Elise smiled because it reminded her of their perilous first date in the snow.

Soon they were at the water's edge. Cerulean's light pierced the surface, the banks of it choked with foliage and brambles. Elise was pulled to a stop.

'What are we waiting for?' she whispered.

Cerulean nodded in front of them. Elise looked into the mist. It was so dense, like standing on a cloud. Without even a whisper of water, a boat pierced the white, thunking against the low bank and bobbing there.

'Where did that come from?'

'I called for it. Come on.'

With ease, Cerulean stepped onto the gently rocking boat and reached a hand out to Elise. They sat down on the hard floor and within moments, the shore was lost to the fog.

'How's it moving?' Elise asked, watching the water churn at the sides of the boat.

'It knows the way.' Cerulean smiled then and held out her arms. Elise went into them willingly, the night's chill creeping over her now that she was still.

'How long until we get there?'

Cerulean cupped her cheek. 'As long as it takes to thoroughly kiss you and erase that anxiety whooshing through your veins.'

For a while, Elise forgot all about magical boats and strange lands. She remembered the bed in the cottage and all the sounds she made as Cerulean touched her, and the ones Cerulean made too. God, she really wanted to do all that again. Maybe not now, not on the boat, but soon, she hoped.

CHAPTER 25

Everything tasted better at midnight, Maddy was sure of it. She stood wedged in the corner of two countertops, spooning out fudge flavoured yoghurt from a pot. All the lights were off, apart from the soft glow of the Christmas tree, spilling its light into the kitchen from the living room. It was illegal to turn on the lights when the Christmas tree was lit—that was Maddy's thinking anyway.

She took another mouthful of yoghurt, telling herself to slow down. It was one of Elise's vegan ones. The pot was tiny and no doubt a million times more expensive than the ones her parent's bought. Another reason not to have the lights on. Less chance of getting busted.

Maddy heard voices in the living room and her hand tensed around the yoghurt pot just as Elise and Cerulean came into the kitchen. She froze with the spoon in her mouth. The two didn't turn on any lights either. No, because Elise was preparing to sneak out. Maddy could see that now, the way the two whispered, the way Elise's movements were slow and careful. In the dark, Maddy tilted her head and watched.

'You'll be warmer in the court,' Cerulean said, making Maddy frown.

Elise didn't reply as she removed her coat from the peg.

Once they'd slipped out the patio door and shut it again, Maddy went to the window and watched them cross the garden. She didn't know what possessed her to put on her coat and shoes and leave the house after them. Probably the two beers she'd just had up in her room.

She waited a while at the garden gate until she was sure she wouldn't be spotted. She took the path leading to the main road, assuming they had too. She spotted them just ahead, holding hands under the streetlights. Maddy's stomach flipped.

When the two turned into the forest, Maddy had second thoughts. If they started getting freaky in the woods, she'd hightail it straight back home. She vowed it to herself.

It was so dark. Maddy yearned to get her phone torch out but that would be game over for sure, so she struggled on slowly. A light suddenly glowed in her peripherals and Maddy looked up from her feet, noticing Cerulean all lit up like the tree in her living room. It reminded her of something Phil had said, the night of the party; the way light flooded from the toilet cubicle Cerulean had entered at Rainbows. Was that the thing, whatever it was? Maddy couldn't figure out where the light was originating from, but it was easing her way.

She thought maybe Cerulean was taking Elise to the cottage she was renting, but they'd already missed the turning for that. They just kept walking and walking. Maddy couldn't remember this particular path being this long but maybe it was the night playing tricks on her. Her eyes were still glued to the two holding hands. It was just so wrong and weird. She didn't think she'd ever get over the fact that Elise was with a girl.

The longer they walked, the more Maddy regretted following them. It was bloody cold out, her coat barely suitable for December temperatures. Her steps slowed and she was just about to turn back when she noticed Elise suddenly stop and peer off into the woods. Maddy jumped behind a tree, heart jolting. When she was sure she hadn't been rumbled, she looked to see what Elise had spotted, and saw some far off lights. She thought she could hear music too. Kinda folksy. Maddy craned her head but she couldn't see anyone out there.

After a moment, Elise walked on with a tug from Cerulean, but Maddy was kind of done. Once they were far enough away, Maddy took out her phone and turned on its torch.

'Why are you following them?'

Maddy spun around at the sudden voice, holding her phone up.

A girl stood there with an arm over her eyes. In her other hand was a box of crackers. 'Can you not?'

'Sorry.' Maddy lowered her torch to the ground, the light bouncing off the girl's shiny Doc Martens. 'You guys having a party out there?'

The girl looked back towards the lights and nodded. 'Taking a breather. What are you doing out here?'

'Kinda stalking my sister,' Maddy said. Sounded weird now she'd said it out loud.

'And the one she's with?'

'Yeah. Her girlfriend. Don't really like her.'

'Because she's fae?' She nodded again, tips of blonde hair brushing her shoulders. 'That's fair. Wouldn't want my sister with one either.'

Maddy frowned. 'One what?'

The girl took a cracker from the box and tilted her head as she nibbled on it. 'You do know she's fae, right?'

'What?' Maddy said again.

'Um, the light?' The girl waved the cracker around her head. 'Ever seen any humans who could do that?'

Maddy looked beyond the girl, down the path she'd just come from. 'Whatever. I'm gonna get off home. I'm cold as fuck. Enjoy your party.'

Maddy began walking. The girl fell into step beside her.

'You don't believe me, do you?' She smirked and held out the box of crackers. 'Want one?'

Maddy took one and bit into it. She frowned. 'What flavour is that?'

'Kale. My fave. What's your name?'

149

'Maddy. You?'

'Abi. So, you don't know your sister's shacking up with the fae? I'm betting she does.'

'Literally don't know what you're talking about.'

'I reckon they're heading down.' Abi took out one more cracker then closed the box and tucked it under her arm. 'That'll be fun for your sister.'

'Down?'

'Where they live.'

Maddy stopped and shined the torch into Abi's face again. 'Do you know Cerulean?'

Abi pursed her lips. 'Never heard of a Cerulean. The gateway's open tonight though. To the court. No doubt that's where this Cerulean is taking her.' Abi's face turned speculative. 'They were pretty hot. Unglamoured too. Lucky sister.'

'Gateway to where?'

'To where they live!' She sounded exasperated. 'Oh my god, it's been ages since I've had to explain this to someone. So annoying.' Abi tucked her head and pinned Maddy with her narrow brown eyes. 'Listen. Your sister's girlfriend isn't human. She's fae. Yes, like fairies. And she's probably taking her below, to where the fae live. Let's hope just temporarily.'

Maddy blinked one, twice, then pointed the torch down the path Elise had just taken. 'Is she safe?'

'Loaded question.'

'But you know where she's going? Can you take me?'

Abi's top lip curled in displeasure. 'I can show you the door.'

'Show me then.'

Abi sighed loudly. 'Fine. Fine, fine, fine.'

They began walking. Well, it was more of a jog for Maddy. She was angsty. After a moment, Abi reached out and pulled at her arm. 'Chill out, will you. So how did your sister meet this fairy?'

Maddy decided to ignore the fairy bit for now. 'At our birthday party a couple of months ago.'

'You two twins? Cool. Well, I'm assuming she's not wild fae or they'd skewer her on sight for trying to get back to the court. Bodes well.'

'What court is this?'

'Unseelie. The low court, the dark court, etcetera. Heard of it?'

Maddy shook her head. 'Nope.'

Abi laughed. 'God. Okay. Total newbie, then. Take it you don't believe in fairies and whatnot?'

'Nope.'

'Cool. Well you will soon. The unseelie court's not far. At least tonight it's not.' Abi waved a hand. 'It's kind of confusing.'

'I've lived next to these woods most of my life. Never heard of it.'

'You kind of have to be in the know.'

'And you are?'

'Yep. My whole life. My mum was involved with one way back. I'm not his, thank god, but I've been exposed to it all since forever.' Abi paused thoughtfully. 'Great way to mess up a kid, to be honest. Ten out of ten do not recommend.' She smirked again. 'Still not believing a word I'm saying, are you?'

'I believe,' Maddy said, 'that you lot are on some seriously heavy shit at that party of yours.'

Abi laughed. 'Well, you're not wrong. Although not me, not again. Haven't been able to eat an apple since, human or otherwise. Literally nothing worse than losing control like that.' Maddy saw her reach up and touch her necklace, made from red beads.

'How long do we have to walk?' she said.

'Not too much longer. Have you noticed how much longer the path is tonight?'

'Why?' she asked.

'We're kind of in a weird in between right now. A space between spaces. That's how my mum described it to me once. It's creepy. You know when you're out somewhere,

151

like in a field or something, and suddenly everything just feels weird, but you can't figure out why? You've probably just stumbled into one of those places, even if just for a second.'

'Sounds fun,' Maddy said because what the hell did you say to something like that?

'Yeah,' Abi drew out, 'super fun.'

In front of her now, Maddy could see the end of the forest path and beyond it, a field clogged with dense white fog. 'Woah,' she said.

'Yep. Come on. Almost there.'

They started across the field. Maddy whipped her phone around, the light bouncing off the wall of fog wrapped all around them.

'Stop doing that. You're making me dizzy.'

'I've literally never seen fog like this. It's mental.'

Abi snorted. 'Just wait for mental.' She peered around. 'The fog isn't usually like this. Means the doorway's closing soon.'

Soon the solid earth turned soggy. Maddy shined the light at her boots, already caked in wet mud. 'Nice,' she muttered.

'Slow down a bit,' Abi said.

Maddy slowed her steps, her boots sinking an inch into the wet mud. A couple of steps ahead of them, the ground dropped off into a body of water.

Abi threw out a hand. 'There's your doorway.'

Maddy peered into the fog above the water just as a white boat appeared from it, hitting the shallow bank at her feet. Maddy stared at it.

'You're saying Elise went on that?'

'I'm assuming that's your sister? And yeah, they went on that.'

Maddy squinted through the fog. 'What's on the other side?'

'The court. You better hurry. You get lost out there and you're basically stuffed. You wanna catch them up.'

'Come with me?'

Abi shook her head. 'Nope. No thanks.'

'Why not?'

'Not for me, that place. Not for you either. Your sister's with someone. Hopefully someone alright. Should be fine. Wouldn't advise it for you though.' She smiled. 'Also can't stop you though.'

Maddy closed her eyes and sighed. Damn Elise. 'I have to,' she said. 'That's my stupid sister.'

The girl shrugged. 'Alright.' She nodded towards the boat. 'That thing will take you there. Just get in it. But wait, before you do—' Abi reached up, pulled the necklace from around her neck and extended it to Maddy. Maddy took it, almost dropping it on contact. The beads were squishy. She turned the necklace over in her hands and saw they weren't beads at all—they were berries.

'What is it?'

'Rowan necklace. New one I made this morning. You'll need it, believe me. Thank me later. If I see you again.' Abi nodded at the string of berries. 'Put it on.'

Maddy did, pulling her hair gently from under it, careful not to squash any of the berries.

Abi watched, her nose crinkling. 'I'm so gonna regret that. Oh well. I better get back anyway.' She lifted her hand in a quick wave. 'Good luck, you loon. Oh, and Maddy?'

Maddy turned but Abi was already lost to the fog. 'Yeah?'

'If things get too weird'—her voice was still light but sounded strange and distant when Maddy couldn't see where it was coming from—'if you get lost, or turned around, just take your clothes off and turn them inside out. Trust me. Just your coat will do. No need to flash the residents.'

The sound of wry chuckling grew weaker as Abi walked further away. Still fingering the necklace, Maddy turned back to the boat before gingerly stepping into it. As soon as she was settled, it began moving.

God, it was eerie. There was no point in even looking around. Everything was just dense white, which was strange considering there was no moon around. It reminded Maddy of the film The Mist and she wanted to kill her brain for deciding to remember that at this particular moment.

She wasn't sure how long she'd sat there, drifting through the damp nothingness, thinking she was possibly dead and heading down the river Styx, when the boat began to slow. The sound of lapping water reached her ears as she arrived at the opposite bank.

The fog wasn't as thick now. It was more like wispy candyfloss. Maddy would've been into it if she had any damn idea of where she was.

She couldn't see Elise anywhere, nor Cerulean. She couldn't see much of anything to be honest. She seemed to be at the back of some garden, maybe. Above her, she could just make out a white balustrade with some straggly grass hanging over the edge of it.

She slowly made her way up the small beach, shoes crunching on the pebbly terrain, and up into the long grass. It was dewy with the same dampness that permeated the air. It was easier to see up here. Maddy stopped beside a tree and took out her phone.

'Crap.'

The time was off and most of her battery had drained. She wanted to bring up her map app and see where she was but didn't dare for fear her phone would die. She did chance a quick call to Elise though, being caught stalking be damned. At this point, she was lost and honestly a bit scared. But the phone just rang and rang.

She was stuffing it back into her pocket when something tugged at her hair. She whipped her head back, eyeing the tree above her. There was nothing there. Obviously. Must have been a branch or something. The fact that there were no branches at head level was something she was willing to overlook.

She knew she was in some kind of garden, and therefore

most likely trespassing, so she kept to the edge of the grass until she found a sagging gate in one of the walls. It was ajar and she pushed it open further and stepped through.

She kept close to the water, feeling safer that way for some reason. The path she was on eventually brought her down onto another beach. The same cotton-candy mist blew through it and in that mist, Maddy saw figures, female ones, lounging in a group on the sand.

Maddy frowned and looked upwards. It was so weird. There was no way it was dawn yet, but the sky, overcast as it was, was fairly bright and tinged with the pink of sunrise.

She began to approach the group, feeling way less rattled than before. They were humming, the women, and Maddy saw they all had mermaid tails instead of legs. Pretty cool. Maddy wondered if it was a manmade beach, one for private use or something, hence why she hadn't stumbled upon it before.

'Hey,' she said. 'Sorry. I'm looking for my sister. Just wondering if you've seen her. Looks like me, just blonde. She's with another girl, also blonde. Taller.'

The humming stopped and all five women peered up at her. This close, Maddy could see the lengths they'd gone to on their costumes. Their skin was painted grey-blue and scaly around their faces. Maddy supressed a shiver at their eyes. They were block blue, the entirety of them.

They still weren't answering her.

'So, have you seem them?' she tried again, feeling more awkward by the second.

The one furthest away lowered her palms to the sand and began dragging herself closer. Maddy forced herself to stay still, at least until the woman grabbed one of her shins and began dragging herself up Maddy's body.

'Um, can you not?' Maddy tried to shake her off but the hands just tightened, pointed nails digging into her skin. 'Ow, get off!'

Maddy raised her free foot and slammed it down on the woman's arm. She shrieked and fell back to the sand, mouth wide in an angry grimace.

'Sorry.' Maddy backed up. In her peripherals, she could see the others slowly bearing down on her. 'But that was your fault.'

Hastily, she left the beach, peering back every second or so to make sure they weren't following her. They stayed on the sand, only following her with their eyes. Wracked with adrenaline, Maddy shuddered. They had to be contact lenses, but god they made them look way more animal than human.

She was beginning to think she was on some rich person's private island. Everyone here was probably on drugs and roleplaying crazy shit to bring back some meaning to their sucky, senseless lives. Cerulean was probably said rich person. It made so much sense. The way she floated around aimlessly, on a different level to everyone else, always grinning and being arrogant as fuck. God, Elise. What the hell was her sister involved with?

She gave the beach a wide berth and the arc brought her to the edge of some kind of beachy woodland, a mishmash of cliff and forest. There was a definite path cutting between the rock, lined with twisty trees. Maddy didn't really want to go down it but it was preferable to whatever she'd just encountered on the beach.

She promised herself she'd just go down to the end of the path and come straight back up again. Hopefully by then the weird mermaid women would be gone.

CHAPTER 26

Elise stood on the balcony of Cerulean's bedroom, looking out over the grounds of the crazy-big house she called home. They hadn't met anyone else yet. Cerulean had rounded the house with Elise in tow, a finger up to her grinning lips, until she reached her bedroom and flew the two of them up to it.

Elise could see others now though. The grounds were thrumming with them. In the muted light, it looked more like a wild orchard than some well-manicured garden. Sticking out of the tall grasses and wildflowers, were rows of trees. Even from this distance, Elise made out apples, pears and plums. How that was possible in the dead of winter, she had no clue. There were bushes too, spotted heavily with bunches of red and indigo berries.

And there were...beings...walking those avenues, some on two legs, others flitting in the air with wings. One of those beings landed close to where Elise's hand rested on the balustrade. She thought it was a dragonfly at first, until she spotted a tiny face peering up at her.

Cerulean swatted it away. 'What are you thinking?' she asked into Elise's ear, trailing a finger down her back.

'That I've gone mad. Or I've died or something.'

Cerulean chuckled softly. 'No, Elise. This is real.'

'Cerulean—' Elise closed her eyes and stepped back into Cerulean's body, seeking the solidity of her. Cerulean's arms came around her tightly and after a moment, she felt steady enough to open her eyes again. 'Oh god,' she breathed. 'Okay.'

Cerulean kissed her neck. Elise remained staring over the strange, misty world, aware of hands pulling off her coat. It was definitely warmer here, Elise thought absently, tilting her head to aid the path of Cerulean's mouth.

Soon those hands were undoing her jeans and pulling them to her thighs. Elise didn't take her eyes of the orchard, only pushed back into Cerulean, her breath releasing with a shaky sigh. She should feel self-conscious, should feel some kind of inkling of shyness, but all she felt was an unusual softness in her mind and total awe at what her eyes were seeing.

There were tears in them by the time Cerulean was done touching her. She turned around and kissed her hard.

'Let me touch you too,' she whispered, eyes falling to the canopied bed in the room beyond.

Cerulean smiled and helped her pull her jeans off the rest of the way before leading her to the bed.

ॐॐ

If she knew how dark the path would get, Maddy never would have taken it. It took her downwards, the rocks and trees on either side twining together to make a canopy above her head. In any other situation, she'd be enjoying the fantastical quality of it but right now it was just plain sinister. What crazy would be cosplaying what down here? Maybe some gay wolf furry. Maddy pushed down a hysterical laugh. At least she'd be in company.

It was hard to think that she was still in Greater Manchester. It felt like another world. She pressed her palms to the boulders as the way became more perilous, snaked with tree roots and tumbling rocks. She must be in some kind of narrow gorge. The walls were caked with moss and heavily cracked where plant matter burst from it.

Maddy hopped onto another rock blocking her path, her

hand slapping at the wall for balance. She stopped for a moment to figure out her next step and glanced absently at her hand, eyes catching onto something. She thought it was just a shadow, a crevice in the rock, but the darkness was moving, like a mass of writhing bees. She snatched her hand back just as a hundred tiny eyes open and blinked at her. She stumbled backwards. The mass began separating but Maddy didn't stick around to find out what into.

She tucked her hands into her armpits and walked as fast as she could until the horrible crawly sensation ebbed.

The path didn't seem to ever end. It was twisty and sometimes when she looked back, she couldn't see the way behind her. That was fine, though. She hadn't taken any hard lefts or rights so the way back would still be a straight shot.

The gorge opened up slightly, allowing in more of the diluted light from above and making her feel less claustrophobic. She heard the sound of tumbling pebbles and scrabbling and noises which weren't quite human, but definitely belonged to something alive. She stopped walking, about to *nope* her way out of there, when something thunked down onto the path in front of her. A second thing thunked down beside it.

They were short, squat creatures apart from their arms which were the longest thing about them. More appeared from the shadows. They walked braced on their knuckles, like disproportionate apes, but without all the fur and brawl; their skin more the texture of rotting wood, sinewy and crackled.

Try as she might, Maddy just couldn't figure out how a whole human could be stuffed inside one of them. Were these kids? She couldn't figure out which was weirder, that the rich bastards were making their kids play like this or the thought that these creatures were real. Which would make Abi right, which would make—no. Maddy just couldn't think like that. She didn't know what that would mean for her sister.

She would just go back home. She'd charge her phone, try Elise again, maybe get her parents involved. She was too out of her depth here.

She turned, but one of the creatures had creeped in behind her. She felt sick with adrenalin now. Whatever they were, they had her trapped. She swallowed hard and braced herself. Chancing it with one, she decided, was still better than a hoard of them. She stepped to the side and made to move past but the creature darted its head out and clamped its mouth around her wrist, pulling away a hunk of her flesh.

She screamed. The creature snarled and hopped forward and Maddy fell right into the rest of them. Too overcome with pain and shock to be coordinated, she struggled fitfully. There was blood everywhere. God, there was so much blood. She held her wrist to her body, eyes blinded by tears.

They pulled at her legs, dragging her along the path and she kicked as hard as she could.

'Elise!' she screamed. 'Cerulean!'

Somehow she managed to get to her knees, and then her feet. She was swarmed, still helpless to do anything but follow them further down the path.

࿐

Elise smiled at Cerulean lying next to her, content with how she'd conducted herself. She'd hoped their second time would be just as smooth as their first and it was. Cerulean seemed pretty easy to please and Elise just couldn't get enough of how smoky her eyes went when she touched her.

Cerulean took her hand. 'Ready to meet my sisters?' Elise tucked her lips and nodded. 'Don't be nervous, moon eyes. You might get lucky and Risarial might be away.'

'What about your parents?'

Cerulean screwed her face up in a way which made Elise smile. 'Father will be with his councilmen at this hour, and Mother her ladies. I couldn't say who will be strategising more.'

160

Cerulean sat up and Elise followed. 'Strategising what?'

'Many a thing. How to further our alliances. To thwart our threats. Dull, dull business I wish to have no part of.'

'So they're pretty high up here then?'

'The highest.'

'Wow.'

Cerulean helped her dress and Elise became aware all over again at just how *bleh* she was right now, her hair greasy, her jeans hems splattered with mud, her underarms still damp.

'I feel gross,' she whispered.

Cerulean shook her head. 'You smell like earth and animal, which is far more favourable than those chemicals that come in cans.'

'Oh,' was all Elise could say to that.

Cerulean opened the bedroom door and led Elise out into the corridor. It was all very white, but not sterile. The walls appeared grey with age and ivy creepers snaked along them, like arrows pointing them the right way. There were tapestries on the walls too, depicting misty landscapes and strange, beautiful looking people. Every few steps was an inset shelf and on those, there were gold-gilded birdcages with creatures inside who looked far too human for Elise to be comfortable with.

'Did you grow up here?' she asked, forcing her eyes away from the cages.

'I did. It's the only home I've known.'

'Apart from your cottage.'

Cerulean squeezed her hand. 'Yes. Apart from that.'

They wended down more beautiful corridors. Sometimes a bird would soar over their heads, tittering a song, or the little creatures in the cages would warble something as they passed.

One of the corridors ended at double doors and opened to a courtyard. The stone floor was cracked, with tiny yellow flowers sprouting upwards. Trees circled an open area in the middle which was dotted with cushions and blankets.

On one of these blankets sat a woman of the likes Elise had never seen before. She was tall and paler than a sheet of paper, with knotted white hair that reached the blanket. She was brushing the hair of a tiny child who sat at her knees. Her fine comb caught in the child's coarse curls and she sighed agitatedly, tugging harshly with the comb. The girl's head yanked with every movement but she uttered no protest. Her eyes were wide, unblinking and trained onto Elise's.

Cerulean cleared her throat and the woman looked up.

'Sister!' She got to her feet and Elise watched the little girl stand up and glide away, the comb falling from her hair and clattering to the stone. It smashed into three pieces but its owner didn't seem to notice. She was too busy staring at Elise. 'You bought your human.'

'Just for a visit.'

'Risarial will fume!'

Cerulean shrugged. 'Elise, this is my youngest sister, Earlie.'

Elise lifted her hand and gave a small wave. 'Hi.'

Earlie offered her a bow, as sloppy as a child's. Elise was fascinated. Her skin was almost transparent, threaded with green and purple veins, but she didn't look sickly. In fact, she looked the opposite. She glowed almost as much as Cerulean did.

Earlie gestured around the courtyard. 'Do you like our home, earthling?'

'It's stunning.'

Earlie turned to Cerulean and pouted. 'Oh, but I miss it earthside. Tell me, have you seen Kenzie?'

Cerulean rolled her eyes. 'No. Now where is Risarial?'

'Here.'

They all turned at the voice. In the open doorway was a woman dressed neck to toe in black. She was easily as tall as Earlie, but her skin was shadowy, with long black hair darkening it all the more. In her hand was a whip.

'Been riding?' Cerulean asked cordially. The woman

162

nodded once. 'Elise, this is my oldest sister, Risarial. Risarial, I bid you be kind.'

'Humans aren't welcome here.'

Cerulean blew out a raspberry and crossed over to a low table holding pitchers of liquid. She poured water into one glass, and wine into another, and handed the one with water to Elise. 'Our sister just had a youngling on her lap. Will you scold her too?'

'That's different.'

Cerulean nodded. 'Oh yes. Of course.'

'You know it is.' Risarial turned her gaze to Elise. 'This one won't be staying.'

'No, she will not.' Cerulean saluted her with her glass. 'Nobody should have to be subjected to you for too long.'

Without another word, Risarial turned on her heel and left the courtyard. Earlie giggled, slapping a hand over her mouth.

'A quiet fume today,' Cerulean grinned. 'We are blessed.'

Elise stood there feeling awkward. She didn't think there'd ever been a time she'd been as openly disapproved of as that. It was almost enough to make her cry.

As if sensing that, Earlie reached out and tugged her hand. 'Come. Sit. Take out your hair tie and let me comb it.'

Elise cringed at the thought of someone touching her hair right now, but she sat anyway, pulling out her hair bobble. Earlie picked up the largest piece of broken comb and began dragging it through her hair.

Cerulean drained her drink and put it down. 'Excuse me. I need to speak with our sister.'

Silence descended upon the courtyard. Elise resisted the urge to fidget, only glad the birds around here were so loud.

'Do you know Kenzie?' Earlie said finally.

'Who's Kenzie?' Elise's eyes fluttered at the gentle touches to her scalp.

'My mortal love. She is in Manchester. Do you know it?'

'Yeah, I live pretty close. Don't know a Kenzie though, sorry.'

Earlie sighed. 'I don't suppose that I'll see her again. That was always the crux of the bargain, after all.'

'What bargain?'

'Our love bargain. Tricky, tricky love. The yearning is enough to drive you mad. Do you yearn for Cerulean?' She gave a light laugh. 'Many do.'

Elise wasn't sure she liked the sound of that. She asked, 'What happened with you and Kenzie? Kenzie was human?'

'Yes. Sweet human. Sad human. Oh, but her friend is here! The boy. Mostly still here.' She put her mouth close to Elise's ear and whispered, 'Do not tell my sisters but I wish for her to come back for him. I wish for her to remember me.'

Elise frowned. 'Why wouldn't she remember you?'

'Requirement of the bargain. As set by Risarial, though heavens knows why. Truthfully, I think she's the saddest out of all of us. Makes me wonder how sad Cerulean will be, when it's time for you to forget her.'

Elise whirled round, eyes smarting at the sudden pain of her hair yanking. She opened her mouth to say something but suddenly Cerulean was there, striding towards them.

'I think I just successfully redirected a tantrum!' she announced happily, pouring herself another glass of wine from the table.

Elise picked up her own glass with shaking hands, holding it tightly as she willed the horrible, foreboding feeling in her chest to fade. Earlie stood up and joined her sister, leaving Elise on the floor, feeling as small and out of place as the tiny child from before.

❧ ❧

Maddy sat slumped on her knees, watching blood from her wrist drip into the sandy, root-strewn earth. She didn't think she'd still be conscious if a vein had been severed but the pain of it more than addled her brain. She didn't know where she was, but she didn't really care. She just wanted the throbbing in her wrist to stop.

They'd forced her into some kind of cave, one which opened up again into a room which was sort of inside, but sort of outside too. Tree boughs created an intricate web far above her head, allowing in weak light. It was enough to see that the place was crawling with creatures. Some sat still in the shadows, looking out from eyes the size of saucers, and others perched high in the branches, wings buzzing loudly against the wood.

Maddy closed her eyes and conceded. These beings weren't human.

The one they'd brought her to leaned forward in her chair and cleared her throat. Maddy opened her eyes and forced herself to focus.

Maybe this one was human, she didn't know. She had all the right parts, but her eyes were a touch too bright for the dimness of the room and shined like amber. The one next to her *definitely* wasn't. She held the same blankness in her eyes as those things on the beach, though Maddy could make out pupils and irises. It was her legs that gave her away. Her feet were resting in a vat of water and a scaly, bulbous tail extended from it, right up until her knees which split into two again. The whole sight made Maddy nauseous.

'Lost are we, poppet?' the amber-eyed woman said. Maddy nodded and the woman clicked her tongue. 'Silly thing.'

'I'm looking for my sister.'

'Two lostlings.' The woman licked her lips. 'Lucky us.'

One of the long-armed creatures creeped forward and batted at her hesitantly. It had red around its mouth and Maddy wondered if this was the one who had bitten her. The amber-eyed woman picked up a large stick and struck it. It bounded away with a shriek. The one with the tail watched it retreat with an absent smile.

'My children are hungry but you wear the beasts' berries.' She put down her stick and reached for Maddy's injured wrist. 'Look at this. You're bleeding all over my lovely floor.'

Maddy cried out. '*Stop,* please. I'm just looking for my sister.' She took a deep breath, and then another. 'Please. She's with someone. One of—one of you. I just need to find her. Then we'll go, we'll leave.'

The woman let go of her arm and Maddy held it against herself, biting her lip hard at the pain.

'Your sister—is she a member of the court?'

'No. But I think the one she's with is. Cerulean.'

The woman glanced at the one next to her and they shared a look. 'Oh, yes? Describe this *Cerulean.*'

'Blonde. She's blonde. And tall. And she kind of—she kind of glows.'

'Like this?'

As Maddy looked on, the woman before her morphed into Cerulean. It was uncanny. She had her hair, the twinkling in her eyes. It only lasted a moment before she turned back. The woman raised an eyebrow and Maddy nodded.

'Yeah, her,' she whispered.

'Hm. Well, this is most interesting.' The woman looked away from Maddy and across at the cavernous room. When she finally looked back, she said, 'I was going to let my children eat you. They have insatiable appetites. Look at them, salivating at the very sight of you. However, I think this would be much more practical. I need you to relay a message to Lady Cerulean. Will you?' Maddy nodded and the woman gestured her forward. 'Come closer.'

Maddy shuffled forward on her knees and the woman bent over her, mouth to Maddy's ear. She smelt of wood and that strange, acrid scent of squashed insects.

'Tell her this,' the woman said.

> *The death of the queen*
> *brings forth a plight.*
> *The death of the king*
> *brings forth the blight.'*

She sat back and regarded Maddy with her strange eyes. 'Can you remember that, humanling?'

Maddy nodded. The words were whirling around her, like the woman was still speaking them into her ear, over and over again.

They were still swirling in her mind even when they'd escorted her out of the cave and through the gorge and back onto the beach; even as she floated back over the water in the white boat now smeared with her blood; even as she fumbled with the latch on the garden gate, almost too weak to push it open.

Elise's bedroom was empty. The sight of it made her crumple into a pile on the floor and sob until she was dizzy. Before she stained the carpet, she dragged herself to her own room and took off her clothes. Naked apart from the necklace of berries, she inspected the wound properly, feeling shaky and faint. It took a long time, cradling her wrist and breathing deeply, to convince herself that she wasn't going to bleed out and die.

She pulled herself up, went into the bathroom and used the small first aid kit in the cabinet to wrap and bind her wound. Thoughts of infection flooded her mind, vying with the woman's voice which still reverberated around and around.

Dawn light was beginning to filter in through the frosted window. How it was almost seven in the morning, she had no idea. She didn't think she'd been out that long. At least her parents would have already left for the day; they had an early train to London that morning. Count on them not to notice that both their daughters were missing.

After ensuring the house was definitely empty, she shoved her bloody clothes into the washing machine and stood against it with her phone in her hand. She brought up Cerulean's number and with her good hand, slowly typed out, *Need to talk to you.*

She closed her eyes. Her head felt cottony and thick. She crossed to the fridge and pulled out a packet of ham, remembering something about eating meat after blood loss.

Taking it back to her room with her, she sat on her bed.

Her hamster was out, noisily drinking from his water bottle. She watched him through hazy eyes, lifting one of the slices of ham to her mouth. She took one mouthful then tossed the rest away, sliding down the headboard until she was horizontal. Sleep was quick to come.

CHAPTER 27

Elise knew they were back in her world when the sky darkened again and the air became frigidly cold. She folded her arms, mostly against the cold but also so Cerulean couldn't reach for her hand. She was feeling weird. She wasn't sure who wouldn't after all of that, but the thing she was thinking about most was the tiny kernel of doubt Cerulean's sister had planted in her.

'Penny for your thoughts?' Cerulean grinned at her, her face all glowy and lit. 'A fair adage, that one. Trading money for one's thoughts. Most fae-like.' Elise smiled back but it was weak. Cerulean put an arm around her. 'I don't have a penny however, so bargain your price.'

Elise frowned at her wording. 'Your sister said something about that. A bargain.' She took in a steadying breath. Confrontation was not her thing. So, so not her thing. She would go crazy, though, bottling it up. 'She said you all set some kind of bargain. That's why you're here.'

'Ah.' Cerulean gave her a squeeze before removing her arm. 'Yes. Risarial's idea. At Earlie's behest.'

'Oh, so you just had nothing to do with it?'

'I never said that. I agreed gladly, I admit it. I'm never one to turn away from a challenge, especially one set by my oldest sister. The thing about bargains though, Elise, is that they're never as straight forward as they appear. Especially ones set by my own kin. I just never imagined I'd succumb to one myself. Never thought I'd be so glad about it, either.'

'What was the bargain?' Elise asked.

'To each travel earthside and find ourselves a mortal lover.'

'That's it? That doesn't sound like a bargain. I mean, it sounds shallow as hell, but don't bargains have, you know, terms or whatever?'

Cerulean nodded. 'Yes. But such terms in this instance could not be revealed until already undertaken. The most dangerous type of bargain to agree to. I believe I am the most fortunate of the three of us.'

Elise walked in silence. Nothing about that was remotely soothing. 'So I'm just entertainment for you? You lot are just going around fetishising us humans?'

'No, Elise. Heavens, no. Those who came before you, maybe. But, no. Not you.' Cerulean stopped and turned Elise around so they were facing each other. Her light ensconced them in a radial glow. Everything outside of it was black. In that moment, Elise couldn't be sure anything else existed. 'Elise, I know I am your first love, first touch, first everything. And in many ways, you are that for me too.' She put a hand to her chest. 'I wasn't even sure this heart could feel the things it does now. That first night, you were naught but a lostling, something to protect and deliver home safely. But heavens, how you became more than that. If I didn't know better, I would think you have me glamoured.'

Cerulean lifted one of her hands, watching the light tinge them gold, veins thrumming with liquid amber. 'My father's family descends from a warrior class,' she said, closing her hand to a fist. 'There is hardly anything of that line left now, bar our trifling party tricks, but when I gaze upon you, Elise, the whole of my being wishes to take you into me, to protect you and cherish you. To hurt what hurts you.'

Her face was so serious, so un-Cerulean. Elise couldn't look away.

'Fae-kind don't love lightly, Elise,' she said, voice low like she was clenching her back teeth. 'Once I give you my everything, you have it forever.'

Elise took her closed fist, turning it over and threading their fingers together. 'What is your everything?' she whispered.

Cerulean smiled. She narrowed the scant inches between them, put her mouth to Elise's ear and whispered into it.

'My name,' she said, pulling back. 'With it, you can bid me to do anything. Anything. I am completely and utterly at your mercy.' She kissed Elise's hand. 'Now and forever.'

Elise looked into her eyes. She turned the name over in her head a few times before licking her lips and saying, along with the name, 'Tell me you love me.'

Cerulean did. After she'd said it, she took Elise by the face and kissed her and said it again, and then again. 'You didn't need my name for that, moon eyes,' she said softly.

'I love you too,' Elise breathed in a rush. Now she was sure nothing existed outside of their circle of light.

She kissed Cerulean back, laughing when she was picked up and spun around and around. She closed her eyes tightly, for once revelling in the dizziness in her head.

CHAPTER 28

Maddy came to consciousness at the sound of the bathroom door slamming out in the corridor. She heard Elise utter an apology along with a little knock to her door. Relief crashed through her, enough to bring tears to her eyes. Elise was okay. Thank *fuck*.

She lay still, trying to take stock of herself without moving. It took a while for her brain to kick into gear. Glowy light was creeping around the edges of her closed curtains, telling her there was probably a really nice sunrise going on, not that she had any intention of seeing it. She burrowed further under the covers. It was Friday, but hell if she was going into college today.

The more she woke up, the louder the woman's voice in her head got, chanting the same rhyme again and again. Maddy forced herself not to panic. Cerulean would fix it, she had to.

A few minutes later, a firmer knock came to her door and then Elise pushed it open. The ends of her hair were still wet and she had her backpack thrown over one shoulder.

'Hey. Why aren't you up?' Elise asked.

'Not going in today.'

'Why not?'

'Period from hell,' Maddy mumbled.

'Oh. That sucks.' Elise glanced around, eyes falling onto the hamster cage in the corner. A smile came to her face.

173

'Still can't believe they don't know about this,' she said, crossing the room and pressing her face against the glass.

Maddy observed her carefully. She didn't seem any worse for wear. Clearly had a better night than Maddy did, at any rate. She didn't even seem mad about having to travel to college on her own. Had she just dreamed the entire thing? If it wasn't for the bandaged wrist she was keeping carefully hidden beneath the quilt, she would have thought so.

'Why are you so happy?' Maddy asked her.

'Just am,' Elise said lightly, that smile still on her face. 'Problem with that?'

'Nope.'

Abandoning the hamster, Elise straightened back up. 'So guess what.'

'What?'

'Mum and Dad aren't going to be here for Christmas.'

Maddy lifted her head. 'What? Serious?'

Elise grinned ruefully. 'Yeah. They just messaged me. There's something going on in New York apparently.'

'On Christmas though?'

'Yeah, I know. New Year too.' She perched on the foot of Maddy's bed. 'Anyway, since we're gonna be here alone, I thought I'd invite Cerulean here for Christmas. It makes sense. She's here on her own too.'

She's hardly far from home, Maddy wanted to say, *and I bet they don't even have Christmas down there.*

But she merely mumbled, 'Fine.'

'Sure?' When Maddy nodded, Elise stood up and said, 'Cool. Well, suppose I better get off. Hope your womb chills out.'

Maddy felt a strange welling of panic watching Elise walk away. She called her back quickly, holding out her uninjured arm. Elise gave her a confused smile but bent over anyway, giving her an awkward hug.

'What was that for?' she asked as they parted, but Maddy only shrugged. 'Okay. Weirdo. I'll see you later then.'

Maddy waited until she heard the front door shut before burying her face into her pillow and groaning loudly. God, her wrist hurt. She pulled it out from under the covers and grimaced at the blood-soaked bandage. She lifted the quilt, seeing the bottom sheet lightly smeared with red too.

Before heading to the bathroom to deal with it, she checked her phone. No answer from Cerulean.

৵৵

The sunrise was stunning that morning. It bled into the bus, blinding Elise with its orangeness. She didn't raise an arm, letting it pierce her eyes and turn everything spotty and distorted.

When she got off the bus, she didn't turn in the direction of her college. There was another bus, two stands down, that would take her into the countryside. Elise boarded it and took a seat on the top deck, where she could ride out the last vestiges of the sunrise.

She felt no anxiety as the bus pulled out, no discomfort at the change in her routine. It took over an hour to get where she wanted to be, not quite in the Peak District but close enough. It was a quiet neighbourhood in the suburbs. She walked along the empty roads until she found a public footpath and took that across a field, towards the hill she could see in the distance. She'd only been here the once, years and years ago, but her body still remembered the way.

At the top of the hill, she sat down, taking out her thermos flask. There was no one around bar a dog walker in the distance. Elise thumbed through her music playlists then leaned back on her hands, grass cold and wet against her palms.

The sky was still cloudless but it held a slightly smoggy quality which reminded her of Cerulean's home. Not that she needed reminding; it was all she was thinking about. She looked out over the fields, the kid's playground she could see in the distance, the train tracks and the metallic smudge

175

of the city in the smog. It all looked so different today. So, so different.

She closed her eyes, remembering Cerulean's words from the night before. God, she was precious. Elise fought back tears at just how much she wanted to hold and love and revel in that strange, wonderful creature.

She sniffed and opened her eyes again, not wanting to miss a moment at what she was seeing even though it was all so ordinary. But it wasn't really, was it? How could anything look the same after having her mind opened, filled with wondrous and impossible things.

Her mind felt whole, that was the only way she could describe it. Every time she'd gone to the woods, yearning to feel even a blip of freedom, every time she'd conjured up anger, just to smother the anxiety—none of that came close to how she felt now. And she knew it would never go away, not as long as she had Cerulean in her life. How could she get het up over such menial things when there was a whole other *world* below hers, and creatures passing between the two of them, and magic and god only knew what else.

A tiny, breathy laugh escaped her. Elise wiped away more tears from her eyes. She wanted to know it all, she needed to know it all.

❧❧

Maddy laid with an arm flung over her eyes, music blasting from her headphones at a concerning volume. Anything to drown out that goddamn voice.

She couldn't hear a thing over the music, which was the whole point, but somewhere around midmorning, the hairs on her arms goosebumped and she suddenly felt watched.

She opened her eyes to see Cerulean leaning against her closed bedroom door. Maddy turned off her music and sat up carefully, still totally drained and not quite with it.

'Hey.'

'Good morning.' Cerulean regarded her. 'Are you ill?'

176

'Maybe,' Maddy said, moving hair out of her face.

After a moment, Cerulean pushed off the door and came to sit beside Maddy on the bed. 'That was reckless,' she said, eyes sparkling. 'Following us like that.'

Maddy stared. 'You knew?'

'Humans are the most unsubtle creatures I've ever encountered. Lumbering animals, all of you.'

'But you never said.'

'Did you want us to know?'

'No, but...' Maddy rubbed her eyes. 'So you...you know that I...know about you.'

'Did Elise tell you?'

'No.' Maddy thought of Abi, wishing she'd bloody prepared her a bit more. 'Someone else.'

'I see. Well? Did you enjoy your visit to the court? I confess I lost your whereabouts shortly after coming ashore.'

Maddy looked down at her quilt, tracing a tear in the thread with her eyes. 'How could you bring her there?'

'What?'

'Elise. How could you bring her to such an awful place?'

A smile creeped over Cerulean's lips. 'You found trouble, didn't you? Trust you. I would be the first to say the courts aren't the safest places for humans to pass through unescorted.'

'Then why take *her*?'

'Elise is safe with me. Always.'

Maddy shook her head. She just couldn't agree with that but she had more pressing matters to deal with at that moment. 'Cerulean, I need to tell you something,' she said, grabbing a handful of her tangled hair and pulling hard. 'She won't leave my head!'

A tiny furrow appeared between Cerulean's eyebrows. 'Who?'

'This—*woman*. One of your lot. Don't know her name but she said—' Maddy took a deep breath and closed her eyes. 'She said, *The death of the queen brings forth a plight. The death of the king brings forth the blight.'*

As soon as she'd uttered the words, the voice fled and Maddy sagged against the headboard in relief. Thank god. She thought she was going mad, that the voice would always be there.

She watched Cerulean for some kind of reaction but she only threw out a dismissive hand.

'Well, what does it mean?' Maddy asked.

'Nothing. Merely an empty threat.'

'She seemed pretty serious.'

'Oh, I'm sure she was. Serious and powerless. There's a lot who feel the same as her, I'm sorry to say.' Cerulean looked to the window and smiled wryly. 'They think we're colonisers,' she said, 'me and my family, since my father was born to another court. He arrived there a hundred years ago, took a mate—my mother—and they've been trying to establish order ever since. Bar a few, they've been extremely successful. But believe me when I say this Maddy—you wouldn't have left the court alive had it not been for my family's hold on it.'

'I almost didn't. They were going to...*feed* me to whatever those horrid creatures were, the ones that did this.' Maddy pulled her bandaged wrist from under the blankets.

The furrow in Cerulean's brow returned, deeper this time. She took Maddy's wrist into her hand. 'Maddy.'

Maddy held her breath. Cerulean sat so close and was touching her and with such concern in her eyes, too. She hated the way her heart jumped.

Cerulean fingered the edge of the bandage. 'May I?'

Maddy nodded, watching as she unwound the bloody material. She looked away when the wound was revealed, instantly queasy.

'It bit me,' she said. 'It was horrible.'

Cerulean turned her wrist over, trailing her fingers over her skin so lightly it almost hurt. 'I can heal this, if you'll let me?'

Maddy nodded haltingly, not sure what she meant.

Cerulean lifted her arm, bringing her wrist close to her face and gently blew on the wound. When she lowered her arm again, the wound was no longer bleeding and it looked a lot shallower. Maddy eyed it with fascination.

'In a few days, it will be healed wholly,' Cerulean assured her. 'That way Elise never need know, yes?'

Maddy looked at her, loathing how pleasant her face was and how all she ever wanted to do was press her body against hers and fall into her. There was no way Elise felt this kind of desire, no way in hell. It was all so bloody unfair.

'Thanks,' she whispered. Cerulean nodded and they lapsed into silence.

'Elise is at college,' Maddy said eventually, balling up the bandage and flinging it in the vague direction of her bin.

'I know.'

'Don't take her to that place again. Please.'

'I told you, she's safe there with me.'

Maddy shook her head. 'I don't believe it. She could just as easily wander off, get lost like I did. If you truly loved her, you wouldn't take her again.'

'And if you truly loved her, Maddy, you wouldn't keep saying what is and isn't good for her.'

'I'm allowed. She's my *sister*.'

'Must you always be so unpleasant?'

'Yes, I must.'

Cerulean sighed, rubbing her thumb against her forehead. 'This isn't what I wanted,' she murmured. 'I didn't want *you*.'

'Well, tough. If you insist on messing around with my sister, you have me to deal with too.'

'She far from needs you, Maddy.'

'I totally disagree. You don't know her. I've known her my whole life. We shared a fucking *womb*.'

Cerulean smiled slightly. 'Do you truly know her, Maddy? Do you truly know who she is in her heart?'

'Yes.'

'I beg greatly to differ. I think you're holding her back

179

from being the woman she wants to be. You stifle her, Maddy. You put her in a box, you closed the lid and you're sitting on it. You've been sitting on it for *years*.' Cerulean grinned. 'But no fear, here I am to pull her from it.'

After a moment of silence, Maddy only said, 'You're really weird, you know that? I don't like you and I don't *trust* you. Leave my sister alone.'

Cerulean chuckled. 'You like me in some ways, Maddy.' She laid a hand on Maddy's knee above the covers. 'Just one advantage fae-kind has over yours is how evolved our senses are. Every spike in your heart, I feel it. Every stirring between your legs, I feel as if it's mine. This isn't about how I treat Elise but everything about me not choosing you.'

Tears sprang to Maddy's eyes. She hated herself for asking, 'Why didn't you choose me?'

Cerulean's careless shrug was like a knife to the chest. 'Who can decrypt the ways of the heart? Elise stirred up in me more than I was seeking when I came here. I never knew such a guileless love could exist.' She glanced at Maddy, as if noticing her tears for the first time and raised a finger to capture one. 'Maddy, you must know that I'm happy to share my body with you, but my heart will always belong to Elise.'

Maddy blinked. 'What? You…you'd do that? Cheat on my sister?' She was repulsed at the spike of arousal that shot through her.

Cerulean tilted her head. 'I don't understand.'

Maddy looked away. She couldn't repeat herself. She didn't trust herself not to—

'Never mind,' Maddy said. 'You should probably go.'

She closed her eyes, not opening them again until she heard that Cerulean had stood up with a sigh and left the room.

CHAPTER 29

Maddy opened the oven, waving away the cloud of heat, and pulled from it her tray of beige. Phil promptly nabbed a chicken nugget but Maddy nudged him away from the pile of curly fries. They were hers.

She nodded towards the fridge. 'There's a couple of ciders in there. Can you get them?'

Whilst Phil plucked the cans, Maddy plated their portions, grabbed some tomato sauce and headed back upstairs.

Music was blasting from her speakers and on the bed were some text books and pens—their shitty attempt at a study night. Elise was over at Martha's for a revision sleepover so Maddy had decided to have one too—with Phil, who had almost less intentions of revising than she did.

She sat crossed-legged on the bed with her plate on her lap. Pointing her fork at Phil, she warned, 'Don't get crumbs on my bed.'

'Try my best.' Beside him, Maddy's phone chimed. He peeked at it before handing it to her. 'Chloe,' he said. 'Didn't know you were still talking to her.'

Maddy snatched it from him. 'Not much.' One-handedly, she quickly messaged her back, eyes drawn, as always, to the pale pink mark on her wrist. Cerulean had been right, it had healed wholly in a matter of days.

As if sensing the direction of her thoughts, Phil asked, 'How are things with you and Cerulean?'

Message sent, Maddy tossed her phone away and began tucking into her food. 'Fine, why?'

Phil shrugged. 'You've just not mentioned her in a while.'

'Shit Phil, it's almost like you want me to still be hung up on her.'

'No, I don't! I'm just checking in.'

Maddy snorted. 'Thanks, but you're not my relationship therapist. I'm dealing.'

'So you're over it now then? Mostly?'

Maddy nodded, not trusting herself to speak. She needed Phil to shut up because she was *this* close to blabbing everything.

When she was done eating, she put her plate on the floor and picked up her English textbook, still unwilling to engage in conversation. She'd hated most everything they'd analysed this year, apart from one poem that she read over now. It was about some girl, not quite human, not quite monster, learning how to love properly with the help of someone named Avery. Her teacher said the someone was a man, but Maddy liked to pretend they were both girls. She hoped this poem would come up on the exam next month anyway.

After making a few annotations, she glanced at Phil who was scrolling through her laptop. 'Dude, you gonna even pretend to revise?'

Phil sighed loudly. 'I am. I'm just—I'm just gonna finish my cider first.'

Maddy rolled her eyes, slamming her textbook shut. 'You are such a bad influence.' She stretched her arms above her head and ran her eyes over her room. 'Hey, you wanna help me bleach my hair?'

'Now *that* is something I can get on board with.'

The whole thing took way longer than it should have. By the time she'd rinsed out the bleach and dried her hair, it was late. Way too late to study anyway. In the bathroom mirror, she eyed her newly blonde hair with pursed lips. She should have left the bleach in a bit longer. It was less white, and more her natural hair colour.

Balling up her now-stained towel, she made her way back to her room.

At seeing her, Phil exclaimed, 'Oh my god, Elise. What are you doing in Maddy's room?'

Maddy rolled her eyes. 'Shut up. I'm still way hotter.' She put a hand to her mouth, yawning loudly. 'I'm wiped. I'll finish dyeing it blue tomorrow, I think.'

'I could sleep,' Phil said. 'Am I in the spare room?'

Maddy waved him off. 'Don't worry about it. The bed isn't made up. You stay here.'

Gathering her phone and pyjamas, she made her way to the office which doubled as a second spare bedroom, the bed in there already made up. She pushed the door open, spotting her dad at the computer, glasses perched on his nose.

'Hey, I want to sleep now. Phil's in my room.'

'I'm still working, Mads.'

'Well, how long are you going to be?'

'A while.' He glanced at her. 'Can't you take your sister's room? She's away tonight, isn't she?'

Sighing loudly, Maddy closed the door and hovered in the corridor. She didn't really want to sleep in Elise's room but it was preferable to suffering through one of Phil's snore fests.

Elise's room smelled of incense. Maddy turned on the light and changed into her pyjamas. Before she got into bed, she messaged Elise to let her know she was using her room. She knew Elise wouldn't care, it was more likely to be her who'd be mad at something like that.

She closed her eyes, frowning at the strangeness of the bed. She'd always hated sleeping anywhere other than her own room. She had always been that kid who had her mum pick her up from sleepovers as soon as it got to bedtime. It didn't help that Elise and Cerulean had probably had sex on this very mattress. God, she hoped the sheets were clean.

She sighed, turning over. A moment later, her phone chimed with a reply from Elise.

Elise: That's cool xx

She dimmed the screen and put her phone back down, just as something snagged her eye at the window. Her breath caught. Cerulean was there.

Maddy blinked a few times to make sure she wasn't hallucinating, but the vision solidified when Cerulean began knocking hesitantly on the glass.

Maddy sat up, then slowly walked over to the window and unlatched it. They stared at each other as cold December air rushed into the room, Maddy's heart thundering in her chest. It beat even faster, knowing that Cerulean could feel it too.

Cerulean smiled. 'Going to let me in, Elise?'

What…? Then Maddy remembered—her hair. She reached up and touched the blonde tips. Surely Cerulean couldn't think that she was—

She stood back and Cerulean hoisted herself over the ledge and pulled the window closed again. Broken light from streetlamps lit her strangely and her skin was speckled with rain. She ran a hand over her face to dry it then kissed Maddy on the mouth.

'Hello,' she said.

Maddy stopped breathing. Cerulean's lips were warm and she tasted like rainwater. She turned away from Maddy and removed her jacket, hanging it over Elise's desk chair.

The look in her eyes, when she turned back, made Maddy want to flee the room.

Cerulean seized her by the waist and kissed her again. 'I've missed you, my love,' she murmured, pressing her lips to Maddy's neck. Maddy felt the touch of her tongue and her eyes slammed shut.

Cerulean's hands burned through the thin fabric of her t-shirt, thumbs stroking over her ribs which expanded with every harried breath she took. She curled her fingers around Cerulean's forearms, ready to push her away. And she

184

would—after just a few seconds more.

Cerulean stepped forwards, herding Maddy towards the bed until she fell over it, legs splayed. Cerulean stood back and began removing her clothes.

Maddy pushed herself up to her elbows. 'Cerulean,' she whispered, shaking her head. ·

When she was naked, Cerulean crossed to the door and locked it, turning back around slowly. Everything inside Maddy clenched. Cerulean's face was grave and if they were in any other situation than this one, she would have thought it was shuttered with anger, not desire.

She came back over to the bed and pulled up Maddy's top, pressing her lips to the feverish skin of her stomach. Maddy tipped her head back.

'Can I remove this, love?' Cerulean whispered, fingering the hem of her top.

Maddy opened her eyes and regarded the ceiling, at the suncatcher hanging there. A second passed, and then another, and then she finally nodded, just once.

Cerulean wasted no time in divesting her of her clothes and laying herself over Maddy. Maddy's arms clamped around her and her jaw clenched at the hot, solid heat of her. God, it was even better than in her imagination.

She accepted Cerulean's mouth on hers but kissed her timidly at first, still at war with herself. She knew there were a million reasons—a trillion reasons—why she shouldn't be doing this but her mind was completely blank, like Cerulean had flicked some kind of switch.

As if sensing her reluctance, Cerulean pushed her hips into her, hard and slow and Maddy knew she had lost the battle. She tangled her hands in Cerulean's hair and kissed her as if her life depended on it. When Cerulean gasped into her mouth, Maddy just about came undone on the spot.

It never felt even close to this with Chloe—her heart beat so fast she was scared it might stop and her lungs refused to take in anything more than quick, shallow breaths.

When Cerulean's hands wandered lower, she had to press her face into the pillow, scared of the noises she might make.

There was no straining for anything this time, her body had taken on a life of its own, coaxed on by Cerulean's steady, determined movements.

As soon as she'd peaked, she reared up and grasped Cerulean, scared that her mind might come back online before she got the chance to touch her. Cerulean's immediate surrender was the sweetest thing she'd ever witnessed.

She never took her eyes off her, some part of her knowing this would be the first and last time they'd ever do this. When Cerulean suddenly gasped and clutched at her, Maddy bit her lip so hard it almost split.

Afterwards, Cerulean settled over her, releasing a soft sigh into her neck. Maddy curled her hands around the arm hooked over her, wanting to stay in this place until all of time had ended. She turned her face slightly, breathing in the scent of her hair. *Clary sage.*

It should have been like this this whole time. Everything was so right, so perfect. Why hadn't it gone like this?

She fought sleep for as long as she could but it was hard when her body felt weightless and still pulsed with pleasant tingles. At some point, Cerulean sat up and kissed her forehead and her eyes didn't open again after that.

CHAPTER 30

Maddy stared into the bathroom mirror, not quite seeing herself. It was the middle of the night and Cerulean was gone, the open window the only evidence that she had been there at all.

Slowly, she roused herself and washed her hands, letting the cold water wake her up. She could see the blonde of her hair in her peripherals and she suddenly needed, more than anything, for it be gone.

Quietly as she could, she crossed the corridor and pushed open her bedroom door. Phil was snoring softly from the bed as she grabbed the tub of blue hair dye and returned to the bathroom.

She was going to mess it up, doing it on her own, but she didn't care. She just couldn't bear looking in the mirror and seeing Elise's face staring back at her anymore.

She sat down on the bathmat and began applying the colour as quickly as she could, uncaring that she wasn't wearing gloves or hadn't lined her hairline with Vaseline first.

As she waited for it to set, she replayed Cerulean touching her, her body stirring again. It was like they'd been made to touch each other, like their bodies just *knew*. She was sure Cerulean had enjoyed it; there was no way she could have faked it like that.

God, she was wicked. Vile. And the worst part of it all was that she didn't feel any regret. Not yet.

Her limbs were stiff when she finally stood up from the floor and turned on the shower. She watched the water run blue, watched it sluice over her body, dripping off her belly bar, the heat and colour of it making her feel like Cerulean still had all her limbs wrapped around her.

She didn't return to Elise's room afterwards. She knew she should probably get the sheets washed somehow but god—she couldn't be thinking about that right now.

Instead she lay down on the unmade sheets in the spare room, knowing they'd probably be stained blue by morning. She closed her eyes. All of her was stained blue now, as blue as Cerulean's namesake, as blue as those sapphire eyes.

She remembered vividly those eyes clouding over, from the blue of a summer's day to the deep blue moments before a storm. She remembered how hot Cerulean was, everywhere she touched her, and all those *noises*—those gasps and grunts.

She parted her lips, breaths coming faster. Her hand twitched at her side. Pretending that Cerulean was still with her, she slipped it into her pyjama bottoms.

CHAPTER 31

From the living room window, Maddy waved her parents goodbye as they got into their taxi, then turned her hand, her middle finger raised. Assholes. She wasn't even mad that they were leaving her over Christmas but leaving her alone with Elise and Cerulean—*shit.*

Maddy had managed to avoid Cerulean in the days since they'd—since they'd spent the night together but it was Christmas eve now and from tomorrow, she'd be here all bloody day.

'We should open our presents now,' Elise said from behind her.

Maddy turned away from the window. 'What?'

'Well, they'd never know.'

On the windowsill, Maddy's phone chimed with a text. She turned back to read it.

'That your girlfriend?'

Maddy frowned. 'Girlfriend?'

'Chloe,' Elise said.

'No, it's Phil. And Chloe's not my girlfriend, not even by a long shot.'

'You got her a Christmas present.'

'So?' Maddy quickly rattled off a reply. 'Anyway, I'm off to Phil's so we can do presents.'

'Cool. Wanna go out afterwards?'

'What?'

'Wanna do something?' From the sofa, Elise smiled at

her and her face was all lit up in a way Maddy wasn't used to seeing. 'I've got the urge to be out somewhere.'

'Since when do you ever have that urge? Shouldn't you be, like, revising or something?'

Elise laughed. 'No.' She shook her head. 'No revision. No stupid college. So do you want to?'

Maddy didn't, she really didn't. Being around Elise at the minute was borderline unbearable. That regret she hadn't felt had crashed into her full force as soon as Elise had got back from Martha's the next morning. It had made the whole thing less of a fever dream, more real. There was just no explaining it away. She had had sex with her sister's girlfriend and was the worst human being to ever have lived.

And for that reason, she couldn't say no.

'Fine. Won't be long at Phil's.'

સ્જ જ

Maddy wiggled back into the orange sofa in Phil's cellar. The whole thing sagged precariously, swallowing you as soon as you sat down, and was the comfiest thing ever. She loved this room. It was like a cave—a posh one—with its own kitchenette and mini fridge. They'd had countless nights down here, watching films on the huge screen and messing around with the jukebox in the corner.

Phil thundered down the stairs with a bag swinging in his hand. He thrust it at Maddy and plopped onto the sofa beside her.

'For you,' he said.

'Thank you.' Maddy pushed her own small pile of presents towards him. 'These are yours.'

She peeked into the bag Phil had given her, spotting blue and white striped wrapping paper. 'Can I open them now?'

'No you cannot. Even you can wait one more night.' Phil placed the bag on the coffee table out of reach. 'So, excited for Christmas?'

'Not really. I think it's going to be really weird actually.'

'How come?'

'Well, my parents aren't here for starters. They've got something on in New York. Not sure what but I know it involves lots of four-course meals at some posh tosser's house.'

'Wow, that's proper shit.'

'Yep. So Elise has decided to invite Cerulean over.'

'For Christmas day?'

'Yup.' Just thinking about it made her heartrate spike. They just had too many secrets between them. One tiny slip up and—

'Can you stop?'

Maddy glanced up. 'What?'

'Jiggling your foot like that.'

'Oh. Sorry.' Maddy pulled her legs under her, resting her head against the sofa back.

'You okay?' Phil asked.

'Yeah, why wouldn't I be?'

'Well, not saying you've ever been normal but lately, I dunno, you've just been more crazy than usual. I've been meaning to talk to you properly about it.'

Maddy frowned. 'Crazy how?'

'Well, you got your belly button pierced. You dyed your hair blue. You got a hamster.'

Maddy laughed. 'Oh wow, I'm so random.'

Phil sighed loudly. 'You're just being impulsive that's all. That's what I'm saying. I just…I dunno, this Cerulean thing is just really getting out of hand. You're getting obsessive. And I know you said you're over all that but you're not, are you?'

Maddy shook her head, eyes on the ceiling light, hoping the tears welling in them wouldn't fall.

'I'm fine,' she whispered. 'All this can't last forever, can it?'

Except it could. Because Maddy knew herself. She knew she got obsessive and she knew her obsessions didn't waver until the object of them disappeared. And Cerulean wasn't going anywhere.

She had never hated herself more.

'Dude, are you crying?'

Maddy dug the heels of her hands into her eyes. 'No, I'm not fucking crying! I'm just pissed off.'

'At what?'

'At me! I just don't know what's wrong with me. I don't know what's wrong with my brain. I don't know why it's like this.'

'Like what?'

'Like—it just latches onto things and just obsesses and never lets go. It's like—fuck, I can't even describe to you how horrible it feels.' She hit at her chest. 'In here. It's just...it's horrible.'

Maddy sniffed a few more times, wiping her nose with the back of her hand. Her makeup probably looked as shit as she felt and there was a headache starting up behind her left eye. She sighed.

'So, I did something bad,' she said.

'What?'

'I might have slept with Cerulean.'

'The *fuck* Maddy?'

'Yeah. I know. I'm awful.'

'But—but why? Like, obviously I know why but oh my god, this is Elise we're talking about. I'm assuming she doesn't know.'

''Course not.'

'When did this happen?'

'Few days ago. Night you were there. She came to the house and obviously Elise was out and it just happened.'

Phil shook his head. 'Are you gonna tell her?'

'Seriously? Do I look like an idiot?'

'Yeah, a fucking big one right now actually. I know you're prone to shit decisions but I'm actually quite shocked at you for this.'

Maddy couldn't take it. She balled her hair into her fists, trying desperately not to cry. It didn't work.

'Fuck,' she gasped, standing up.

'Where are you going?'

Maddy just shook her head and stalked back up the stairs.

᠀᠆᠀᠆

Elise stood looking up at the coffee shop menu, amid the nutty aroma of roasted beans and the loud hissing from the milk steamer. The shop was packed but she didn't mind. They were playing Christmas songs and someone had brought in their puppy and the other patrons were taking pictures of it and asking for cuddles. It was all so cosy and sweet.

When it was her turn, Elise ordered two lattes and cakes from behind the counter. She knew Maddy was watching her. It was unusual that she was the one to order for them. Usually her anxiety forbade her, but today her mind was mellow. There was nothing scary here, not anywhere.

She walked back to their table with the tray.

'I got you a brownie. It's vegan. Hope you don't mind.'

Maddy pulled the plate towards her. 'Chocolate's chocolate.'

Elise had gotten herself a slice of lemon drizzle cake. She cut a piece off with her fork. It was sour on her tongue, the glaze so thick it crunched.

'You can't even tell,' she said, holding her hand under her chin to catch any crumbs. 'You'd never know that was vegan.'

'Brownie's not bad either.' Maddy looked around the coffee shop. 'Do you think they go crazy here? Always playing the same Christmas songs.'

Elise smiled. 'I know I wouldn't. I'm actually quite excited for tomorrow. Are you? We can do whatever we want. We don't even have to have Christmas dinner if we don't want to. We can eat whatever.'

'You just don't want to cook the turkey.'

Elise laughed. 'True. My first vegan Christmas.'

'So what—just vegetables?'

Elise shrugged. 'Fine with me. Roasties are the best thing about Christmas dinner anyway.'

'Agreed. What about Cerulean, is she vegan?'

'No. I know one of her sisters is. She eats kinda…healthy though. Lots of stews and salads and stuff. Cottagey things.'

'How long she's staying there for?'

'Dunno. She says she's not really thought about it. Just going with the flow.'

Maddy nodded slowly. 'Must be nice, being able to live like that.'

Elise smiled wistfully. 'Yeah. I'm kinda…I'm kinda hoping I get to live like that. You know, with her.'

Maddy pushed some of the brownie crumbs around on her plate. 'That serious, then?'

'Yeah.' Elise nodded. 'Yeah, it really is. I know it's early days but I just have a feeling about her, you know? The kind of feeling where you just *know*. She really, really loves me.' Elise drew in a breath. 'It's so nice…and—*god*, it's so hard to explain. I wish I could. I wish I could—' Elise shook her head. It felt like her brain was bubbling over, like it was too small to contain all of *this*.

In front of her, Maddy sat up, fidgeting slightly in her seat. 'Elise, I know about her,' she said.

'Huh?'

'I know about her…you know, not being *human*. Being…whatever she is.'

'Oh.' Elise looked into her cup, tracing the frothy, spidery designs on the inside of it. Maddy knew? 'How? She told you?'

Maddy nodded. 'Yeah. Kind of. I cut my wrist and she said she could heal it. It all kind of came out then.'

'You cut your wrist? Like on purpose?'

'No! It was an accident. Pretty bad though. She did something and it closed up.'

'Let me see.'

Maddy put her arm on the table and lifted up the edge of her sleeve. Elise took her wrist and twisted it so the light hit it better.

'When was this?' she asked. There wasn't much there now, just a pale pink mark and a couple of shiny white dots that looked like years-old scars.

'The other day. That day I had bad period pains. She forgot you were at college and dropped by.'

Elise let her eyes drift over to the window as she digested that. The glass was steamed up from the inside and the people walking past the coffee shop looked spectral, faces blurred and limbs all blending together. She often found herself wondering if anyone out there was fae too. She knew they could disguise themselves. Cerulean had told her that. The fact that she'd also told Maddy these things sat strangely with her. She kind of liked being the only one to know these things. It made her feel special and...chosen, in a way.

But now Maddy knew too. The girl she used to tell all her secrets to. When had they stopped doing that? She felt a sudden spike of excitement.

'It's mad, isn't it?' she whispered, biting her bottom lip.

Maddy snorted. 'Yeah, it's mad.'

Elise leaned forward. 'Yeah but Maddy, she's not *human*.'

'Yeah, I get it.'

'It's mad! Everything we know about the world is just wrong. There's so much more out there and god, I'm so excited to see it all. It's like nothing matters anymore. None of the normal stuff.' She looked at Maddy with gleaming eyes and said, 'I'm quitting college.'

'What?'

'Well, not quitting exactly. There's only a few months left. But I just don't care about it that much anymore. It just feels so pointless. I'm quitting therapy too. I emailed them this morning.'

'Elise, don't be stupid.'

'I'm not!' Elise leaned back in her chair, eyes finding the tiny puppy who was now asleep on its owner's lap. 'I just feel like a completely different person. It's mad that nobody else knows this stuff. Do you reckon the government does? I bet they do. Just keeping it all a secret. Probably for the best to be honest. It might put Cerulean and people like her in danger.' Elise closed her eyes. 'God, I'm so glad I met her. Aren't you?'

'Yeah. But Elise…they're not all like Cerulean, you know. Some are worse. Like, really bad.'

'What do you mean?'

'I mean, where she's from. The court. Some of the creatures there are evil.'

'She told you all this?'

Maddy nodded.

'Well, I'm safe with Cerulean,' Elise said. 'More than safe. Just look at the size of her! Oh, I'm actually quite glad you know all this. It's like when we were kids and made up those witch women. Oh my god, we went into so much detail, made up a whole world. And that one time I told Mum about them and you got into such a strop with me! Like I was spilling real secrets.'

Maddy smiled slightly. 'Yeah, I remember. But this is real, Elise. Real sometimes isn't as nice.'

Elise rolled her eyes. 'You sound like me. All serious and worried. Have we had a brain swap or something? I can't believe you didn't tell me you knew. You haven't told anyone have you?'

'No.'

'Not Phil?'

'No one.'

'Good. Let's not.' Elise's eyes gleamed. 'You know our lives are changed forever, don't you? The world is so much bigger now.'

CHAPTER 32

Maddy sat in front of the Christmas tree, knees pulled up to her chest, listening to the ticking of the grandfather clock on the wall behind her. It was Christmas morning and the house had never been so quiet. Elise had stayed at Cerulean's cottage the night before and Maddy kind of wished they'd remain there and let her be alone. On Christmas.

Maddy buried her face in her knees and snorted. She was pathetic. Seriously, truly pathetic. She'd never had a great relationship with herself but now the self-loathing was truly spectacular. What she'd done was eating her from the inside out. And now she got to spend the *whoooole* day with the two people who were responsible for her feeling this way.

Still, it wasn't all bad. Their parents had clearly felt guilty for abandoning them on the holiday so they'd generously stocked the minibar with enough booze to flatten an army. Maddy picked up one of their stupid little crystal glasses and filled it to the brim with mulled wine. She didn't have it in her to go warm it on the stove first.

When she heard the backdoor slide open and the burr of voices, she drew in a bracing breath, tonguing away the spiced wine taste from her teeth.

Elise came into the living room with a smile on her face. 'Merry Christmas! Did you put the turkey in the oven?'

'No. Was I supposed to?'

Elise tutted. 'Not going to cook itself, Maddy. Takes a

couple hours in the oven. Can you go preheat it please? I want to get changed into something nice.' She started up the stairs. 'And for god's sake Maddy, get dressed!'

Maddy rolled her eyes.

Flopping down on the sofa beside her, Cerulean grinned. 'She's excitable today.'

'Yeah.' Maddy twisted the empty crystal in her hands. 'She's always been obsessed with Christmas.'

Her heart was thudding and she smothered a sigh because she knew Cerulean could sense it and she hated that. It was such a violation. How could Elise put up with it? Did she even know?

She shifted on the sofa. This was so awkward. She had the mad urge to bring it up, to clear the air, but it was possible Cerulean didn't *know*. To her, she had slept with Elise, not Maddy. That was the bit that messed her up the most.

'What a strange tradition,' Cerulean said, coming to squat in front of the Christmas tree, 'to put gifts beneath a felled tree. To whom do you make these offerings to?'

'No one,' Maddy said, feeling better now that Cerulean's back was to her. 'There's a guy called Santa—it's a whole thing. Get Elise to explain it.'

'But I asked you,' Cerulean replied, giving her a strange look as she returned to her place beside Maddy. 'I brought gifts too.'

'Yeah?'

'I thought, since the two of you are aware of my nature now, and aware that the other is aware too, I'd bring gifts from my home for the both of you.'

Maddy nodded. She didn't like the way Cerulean had said that twisty sentence, lumping the two of them together like that. It felt like a bind, one she wanted to free herself from.

Standing up, she headed back to the minibar.

'Want some mulled wine or anything? My dad bought some orange whiskey stuff too, if you fancied that.'

'Wine would be nice.'

'Cool. Want me to heat it up for you?'

Cerulean shook her head. 'Why do you humans do that?'

Maddy glanced at her. 'What, don't have mulled wine where you're from?'

'No. This is a truly human holiday.'

'Alright.' She poured the wine into another glass. 'Have it cold. Save me a job.' She handed the glass over. 'I should probably go get changed too.' She gestured towards the minibar as she passed it. 'Help yourself to more. There's stuff in the fridge too.'

֍֎

Maddy stayed in her room until Elise finally smoked her out, calling her downstairs.

'Don't think you're hiding in your room all day,' Elise told her. She was setting out finger foods on the kitchen table, placing them strategically around the candles, fake ivy and holly garlands. Maddy had to admit it looked great. At the head of the table, Cerulean sat folding napkin swans. 'Turkey's in the oven. You're welcome, you carnivores. It'll be stinking the place out soon.'

'This time last year you'd be tucking into it along with the rest of us.'

'Yeah well, a lot can change in a year.' She sent Cerulean a meaningful look and Maddy resisted the urge to shove her fingers down her throat.

'So, when are we opening presents?' she asked, picking up and biting into an almond-stuffed olive.

'Maybe before dinner? Since it's going to be ready a bit later. Thought we could do some boardgames first?'

Maddy nodded. She could handle boardgames. 'I'll go get them out the cupboard.'

A few minutes later, she was sat on the living room floor, Christmas music playing softly from her speakers, setting up a game of Monopoly. Her token was always the dog, and she set that down on Go next to the thimble Elise always chose. She wasn't sure what Cerulean would pick or even if she knew how to play Monopoly. She doubted they had it where she was from. Human sacrifices were probably more their speed.

'This looks like a fine game,' Cerulean said. She plopped down on the opposite side to Maddy, fingering the piles of money tucked under the edge of the board.

'Pick your piece.' Maddy pushed the box towards her. Cerulean hesitated a moment before picking the top hat. She placed it down on the board, between the dog and the thimble.

'Almost done!' Elise called from the kitchen.

Cerulean stretched out, the loose fabrics of her weird clothes getting trapped beneath her, tightening on her thick arms and thighs. Maddy stared. Her mind was muzzy from the mulled wine she'd drank and it was throwing her flashbacks from the other night, ones she'd sworn to stop thinking about. She remembered those arms, how they came all the way around her like she was merely a doll. She remembered those lips, those pink, pouty lips, kissing her torso, licking each of her ribs.

When she managed to draw her eyes away, Cerulean was looking at her. For once, her mouth wasn't smiling.

'Okay,' Elise breathed, tossing a kitchen towel to the sofa. 'I'm ready.'

Cerulean picked up the rules of the game quickly and she took great pleasure in seizing as many properties as she could. She was ruthless; even Elise looked startled. In hardly any time at all, the two of them were bankrupt.

'Beginner's luck,' Maddy said flatly, pushing the metal dog over onto its side.

'Wanna play something else?' Elise asked.

'No, I want to do presents.' Maddy shuffled over to the tree. The first couple of presents she picked up were for Elise and she put them into their own pile. She did the same for hers, and Cerulean's, until the only presents left beneath the tree were the ones her and Elise had bought for their parents.

'We should burn them,' she said, nodding to the gifts.

'We should not. I spent loads on that thing for Mum. I thought they'd take a couple with them at least.'

Maddy watched Cerulean approach her own pile, a slightly bemused expression on her face. She touched the cloth bag of the gift Maddy had bought for her, and a flush rose to Maddy's cheeks. She would have felt like a dick if she hadn't bought her *something* but now she found herself hoping Cerulean would actually like it.

'What do we do now?' Cerulean asked.

'Rip into the suckers,' Maddy said, proceeding to do just that.

Elise did so more slowly. She had what she termed 'present anxiety'. Maddy didn't understand how you could be nervous opening presents from other people—surely it should be the other way round?—but it was on character for Elise.

Finally, the only gift she had left was the one from Cerulean. It was in a small drawstring bag, embroidered in gold with some crest. It looked like a being with many wings, much like the petals of a lotus flower.

Maddy opened the bag and upended it onto the carpet. It was some kind of medallion, with a flat, milky white stone set in the centre of it. Maddy ran her thumb over it and the stone became hot.

'It's a touch stone,' Cerulean said. Maddy looked up. Elise was holding an identical medallion in her own palm.

'It's burning,' Elise said.

'Yes. It grows warm when the other touches their stone and vice versa.' Cerulean smiled. 'They're twins, like you.'

Elise peeked up at Maddy, then pressed her thumb to the stone. Maddy felt hers heat.

'That's cool,' Maddy said. 'What's the distance on it?'

'All distances bar death.'

'This is fae magic?' Elise asked.

Cerulean inclined her head. It was the first time they'd

all acknowledged Cerulean's nature and the moment was strangely heavy. They sat in silence for a few seconds, Greg Lake crooning behind them, before Elise pulled herself over to Cerulean and kissed her cheek.

'That's super sweet, thank you.'

Cerulean nodded. 'I would also like to extend an invitation to you both. In six days' time, there is to be a revel in the woods close to here.'

'Like a New Year's Eve party?' Elise asked.

'I believe it is to hail in your new year, yes.'

'Cool. Well, I don't have any plans.' Her eyes flicked to Maddy's. 'How about you? Fancy it?'

Maddy pursed her lips. She did not. She and Phil usually had plans, but her mind was suddenly conjuring up images of a whole swarm of fae creatures and Elise thrust in the middle of them all and she knew she couldn't abandon her to it. 'Yeah, I'll go.'

Cerulean inclined her head again. She took hold of the gift from Maddy and shook it, shooting her a smile.

'You got her something,' Elise said, surprised. She put her fingers to her mouth as if realising what that sounded like.

Maddy frowned. 'Yeah. Be rude not to.'

Cerulean opened the bag and caught the figurine that tumbled from it. It was a turquentine bird, wings outstretched and bearing the sun on its back. Maddy found it at the weird hippy shop near college and had bought it immediately.

'It kind of reminded me of you,' Maddy said, not meeting her gaze.

'Blue like your eyes,' Elise put in gently.

Cerulean turned it over in her hand, then closed her fist around it as if she was warming it. She looked up at Maddy, a soft smile on her face.

Maddy looked away. She stood up and relieved her dad's whiskey from the minibar.

There was too much in that smile, too much she wanted

and had no right to want. She poured a tiny amount of the spirit into a glass, closing her eyes at the horrid burn.

Behind her, she heard Cerulean opening her gifts from Elise. She took another swallow and tuned them out.

࿆ ࿆

By the time they'd eaten dinner, Maddy's mood had darkened. She'd hoped the copious amount of food would sop up some of the alcohol she'd imbibed in throughout the day but it did no such thing. She felt buzzed and reckless, and afraid of what she might say or do—accidentally or not.

She sat huddled on one sofa, her Christmas jumper pulled down over her knees as they watched *Home Alone*. Elise and Cerulean were curled up on the other, limbs entwined. Maddy pulled her hair down over her eyes like a faded blue fog until she couldn't see them.

She watched the rest of the film like that, hair obscuring her vision like some grunge filter.

'Oh guys!' Elise exclaimed when it had finished. Maddy lifted her head. 'We didn't do the crackers!'

She bounded into the kitchen. Cerulean glanced at Maddy, eyebrows raised.

'Crackers,' Maddy said. 'It's a tradition thing. You pull them, they bang, and you get a shitty gift. And a crown. Don't know why we do it.' Maddy waved a hand as if dismissing the whole thing.

'It seems to me, you don't know much of why you do what you do,' Cerulean replied, watching Elise return with the box of crackers.

For some reason, the comment pissed Maddy off.

'Here.' Elise handed them both a cracker. 'We can even do two each if we want, since Mum and Dad aren't here.'

'One's enough,' Maddy replied.

'Shall we do the thing?' Elise crossed over her arms, demonstrating.

Reluctantly, Maddy joined them by the sofa.

'Like this Cerulean,' Elise instructed. 'Grab Maddy's cracker in your other hand. That's it. Now pull.'

Cerulean jumped when the crackers snapped and Maddy laughed. 'Your face,' she snickered.

Cerulean shook her head, smiling, and glanced down at her cracker half.

'Wow, we all won,' Elise said. She nodded towards Cerulean. 'Tip it out. See what you have.'

Maddy pulled free her crown and shoved it on whilst unwrapping the small sliding puzzle. It featured a snowscape and a shoddily rendered Rudolph.

She looked at Cerulean who held a metal toenail clipper between two fingers. After a moment, she hissed and dropped it to the sofa.

Elise eyed it. 'Oh my god. Metal burns you.'

'Only some.' Cerulean wiped her hand down her trousers. 'Let me make a trade.' Scooping the clippers back up, she dropped them into Maddy's lap. 'Your nails are most feline,' she said, pulling the sliding puzzle from Maddy's hands.

Maddy fingered the clippers, remembering acutely her nails digging into Cerulean's back that night, no doubt leaving red lines all along those defined shoulder blades. She peeked up at Cerulean who regarded her with a look she didn't dare try to decipher.

'Well, I'm chuffed with my fish,' Elise said, peering at the piece of red, paper-thin plastic on her palm. The fish remained motionless, even after she gave her hand a shake. 'Oh, I'm dead.'

'Far from,' Cerulean said, tossing the fish away. She wrapped her arms around Elise and that was Maddy's cue to return to her own seat.

She pulled her hair back down over her eyes as she flicked through the TV channels. Even partially blind, she could still hear perfectly—Cerulean's breathing, every wet kissing noise, Elise's low chuckles. And all the while, Cerulean twirled the bird Maddy had gifted her in her fingers.

At some point, Cerulean must have dropped it because suddenly it was pinging off the carpet, landing just in front of the Christmas tree. Maddy followed the path of it, feeling very far away.

'That really is the exact blue of your eyes,' she murmured.

'Blue as that jewel in your belly, too,' Cerulean said, tipping her a wink as she retrieved it.

Maddy's heart seized, because there was only one time Cerulean could have seen her belly bar...

Sitting up, Elise frowned. 'You got your belly button pierced?' Maddy nodded slowly. 'When? Let's see.'

Unfurling herself, Maddy lifted her jumper, letting the lights of the Christmas tree glint off the fake jewel.

'Oh, I like it,' Elise said, leaning over to get a closer look. 'Might get mine done. Did it hurt a lot?'

'Just for a second.' Maddy dropped her top and fished around for a subject change. 'Anybody want dessert? There's that trifle, and the Christmas cake.'

Elise put her arms into the air and stretched. '*Mmmm*, I might have a mince pie. The rest aren't vegan.' She jumped up from the sofa. 'But first, I have to pee.'

Maddy got up more slowly, unsteady on her legs. The lights in the kitchen made her squint. She pulled a couple of mince pies from the box and shoved them into the microwave.

Beside her, Cerulean sidled up, sliding three plates onto the countertop. Maddy's eyes flicked to her.

'Stop it,' Maddy said.

'Stop what?'

Maddy threw up a hand. 'Inferring shit. She's not stupid.' She folded her arms and took a breath. 'So, you knew it was me then.'

Cerulean gave her a look. 'Maddy.'

'Then why did you?'

'Why did *you*?'

205

Maddy put her hands on her head. 'God, this is so messed up.'

Cerulean tilted her head, a perplexed smile on her face. 'Why does this trouble you so?'

Maddy stared at her. 'Seriously?' She shook her head. 'Look, just don't let Elise know about this. *Please.*'

Maddy turned on her heel to leave but Cerulean caught her wrist. Frozen, she peered up at Cerulean who stepped closer, an enigmatic smile on her lips.

'You were magnificent,' she murmured, breath ghosting over Maddy's face. 'That night. So different from Elise—'

Maddy wrenched back her wrist. She shot Cerulean a glare that could kill and stormed out of the kitchen.

She blew past Elise coming back down the stairs. 'Thought you were getting the mince pies?' she asked.

'Get them yourself,' Maddy snapped.

శ౷

Maddy stared up at the bulb of her bedroom light. It still glowed faintly, even though she'd turned it off minutes ago, and it was the only remaining light in the room. It wavered in and out of sight as Maddy cursed herself for getting so drunk. The room was spinning. She was fine now, but she knew she'd be puking come morning.

She heard a noise from somewhere else in the house and her eyes flicked to the door. It wasn't locked. Maddy always locked her door before sleep. That she hadn't tonight was something she didn't care to dwell on.

She licked her dry lips, wishing she'd brought a glass of water up with her earlier. She was feeling shitty, still remembering Elise's quiet nod when she said was turning in for the night. She'd hoped Elise hadn't noticed her bad mood but Elise noticed most things. Maddy closed her eyes against the guilt. First, their parents abandoned them, then she decided to subject Elise to her foul mood all day. And her sister loved Christmas…

Maddy heard a squeak: the handle of her door pushing down. On the bed, she froze. For a second, a body was backlit in the doorway before it closed again, plunging the room back into darkness.

Maddy sat up, instantly on the defence.

'What are you doing?' she whispered harshly.

The bed dipped as Cerulean sat down. Maddy couldn't see her eyes in the dark. It strangely frightened her. 'Maddy.' A fingertip travelled up her arm, making her shudder. 'You've been distracting me all day, do you know that? I've felt your mind on me, even when you weren't looking. Your heart beating out of rhythm, your blood heated. And heavens, the smell of you.'

Maddy broke away. 'Get off.'

'I want you too tonight.'

'Are you actually for real?' Maddy hissed. 'Elise is literally in the room opposite us. You know, your *girlfriend*.'

'She won't wake, Maddy. I've made sure of it.'

'What do you mean, you've made sure of it? What have you done to her?'

'Nothing close to what you're thinking, I'd imagine.' Her voice was murmuring, slow. 'You humans are very suggestible. It doesn't take much doing to put you into a deeper than deep sleep.'

'Well, do that to me then and get the hell out.' Maddy turned over and laid with her hands over her head.

'Do you truly want that?'

'No,' Maddy whispered. 'You know what I want. You know I can't have it. And it's beyond fucked that you're doing this to the both of us.' Maddy bit her lip, fighting tears. 'So just get out.'

For a moment, the room was so quiet it was almost like she was alone again.

Then Cerulean sighed. 'It vexes me, to hurt so unintentionally. Until now, I have always hurt with a purpose.' The bed rustled as Cerulean stood back up. Her last words before she left the room were soft, 'I fear I am truly out of my depth in this realm.'

The door clicked shut. Maddy jumped out of bed and locked it. She faced the dark room, shaking with an emotion she couldn't name.

Closing her hand to a fist, she struck her mattress.

'*Fuck!*'

CHAPTER 33

In the kitchen, Maddy sat cross-legged at the table, a bowl of cornflakes in front of her. When she last ate a spoonful a few minutes ago, the cereal had been soggy. She didn't want to know what they'd taste like now.

She held her phone in both hands, messaging Phil. She felt like a dick. He'd been stoked about New Year's Eve, wanting her to finally meet the boy she'd forgot he was dating. He had tickets for some club in Manchester. Oh well. She'd make it up to him. She needed to be at the revel tonight. If there was any chance those assholes from Cerulean's court were going to be there, then so would she. Elise might be in love with a fairy but it was clear she didn't know the first thing about them, not in the way that Maddy did.

Phil sorted, she dumped her cornflakes in the bin and freed a slice of stale Christmas cake instead. She was going to need all the energy she could get her hands on for tonight.

❧ ❧

She put down her mascara and regarded herself in the mirror. She'd gone a little heavier on the black makeup tonight, matching the black boots, jeans and jacket she was wearing. She'd even dyed her hair dark again, having come to hate anything blue with a passion. Something about all the black made her feel powerful, older. She remembered all too vividly how scared she'd been in the unseelie court and wanted to make sure she felt the opposite of that tonight. The only point of colour on her now was the necklace Abi had given her. The berries had shrivelled up to almost nothing and were the colour of old blood.

She'd been mentally preparing herself all day but now it was almost time to leave, she felt high on nerves. Her foot wouldn't stop jiggling. Picking up a can of vodka mixer from her desk, she took a swig, trying to lose herself in the dark music roaring from her speakers.

Elise and Cerulean were getting ready in her room. Well, Elise was. Cerulean had come ready. She wore a pair of black breeches, a loose-fitting grey shirt tucked into them and pointy, shiny shoes. She looked like some renaissance-era nob. Maddy had told her so but Cerulean had only smiled wickedly—she knew exactly what Maddy really felt.

Maddy bagged up her makeup and went downstairs to wait.

❧ ❦

Elise bit her lip as Cerulean's hand slowly disappeared under her dress, rubbing at her underwear. Part of her wanted to push her away, another to grasp her wandering hand and press it against her harder. They didn't have time for this. Maddy was ready, as signalled by her music turning off, a loud rap at her bedroom door, then the sound of her thundering down the stairs in her boots.

But god, Elise was near powerless to stop her.

'Cerulean,' she whispered.

'Mm?'

'It's time to go. I still need to put on my tights.'

'No need. I'll keep you warm.' Cerulean's hand dropped from her anyway. 'I'll wrap you up in my heat. It'll be like we're embracing all night.'

Elise smiled. She stood on her tiptoes and kissed her. 'Can't wait to do that with you at midnight.'

'I think I will enjoy that silly tradition.'

As they walked down the stairs, an incredible heat came over her, like she'd been dumped into a furnace and someone had shovelled in the coals. She swayed on the stairs. The heat was everywhere, especially in the place she was trying to ignore after Cerulean had stirred it up.

'Turn it down a little,' she breathed.

When she was steady enough, she continued down the stairs.

చ్ ఆ

Maddy walked a few paces behind Elise and Cerulean, feeling like an invisible and slightly menacing shadow. Her eyes darted through the trees, senses heightened in the dark. Her hand was frigid around another cocktail can.

The forest path was endless and Maddy knew they'd wandered into an in-between place. It wasn't long then until she heard that strange music and spotted lights bobbing through the trees. Elise and Cerulean stepped off the path. With a breath, Maddy followed.

The clearing hosting the revel was surrounded by trees, their trunks bent outwards as if held at bay by some unnatural force. In the middle was a fire and it crackled loudly, spitting orange embers into a sky which held far too many stars. Maddy craned her head upwards, a shooting star whizzing over her head. She didn't bother with a wish; it wouldn't come true.

There were lots of bodies in the clearing but Maddy refused to look at them as Cerulean cut a path to a table standing at the edge of it. It listed on its side, the thick wood cracked and damp. There were numerous liquids atop it— alcopops, cans, weird glass bottles that seemed to glow and prismed-glass bowls of deep coloured punch. Next to one bowl, a human-looking boy dropped a six-pack of lager. He wrestled one free, giving them a nod as he rejoined the party.

Maddy put down her empty cocktail can and swapped it

for an alcopop. Beside her, Cerulean picked up a frosted, ornate bottle and the glass glowed pink at the touch of her fingertips.

'Fae wine,' she said, noticing both her and Elise's inquisitive looks. 'Cultivated in the wineries of the seelie court. Their summers are endless; their fruits begrudgingly superior.' Elise reached out to take it but Cerulean pulled it back. 'I must warn you, moon eyes, this will affect you far more than it will me.'

'Never take fairy food,' Maddy said, as if remembering something from the back of her memory.

Cerulean smiled and took a swig. 'Never say never.'

'Elise, just have a cider, look.' Maddy took a can and pressed it into her hands.

Elise flicked the top of it open and leaned back on the rickety table, looking out over the clearing. 'This is so cool,' she said, eyes bright. 'I feel like I've just walked into some fantasy tavern or something.' Maddy nodded but kept her eyes averted from her surroundings. 'Do you know anyone here, Cerulean?'

Taking another swallow of her wine, Cerulean shook her head. 'No, but a few might know me.'

'Because you're a bigwig back home?' Elise teased.

Cerulean kissed her head. 'Exactly.'

Maddy wanted to get out of the light. It was kind of hard with Cerulean glowing but she still felt better when they'd wandered over to the boundary of trees. Finally, Maddy let herself look around.

The band played on the other side of the fire. There were six musicians, all squat, rotund creatures, their hands flying surprisingly quickly over their instruments. In the air just above their heads, tiny, lit-up beings flittered about. Maddy would have thought they were fireflies if they had those in this abundance in this part of the world. One of the musicians turned towards the firelight and Maddy saw an extended stomach. She looked into the creature's face but still couldn't tell if they were male or female.

A tree canopy near her rustled and Maddy looked up, spotting the inhuman glow of eyes there for just a second. A female creature jumped onto the trunk of the tree below, her bald head cocked upwards. She scaled the tree with the grace of a lizard. It was creepy, reminding Maddy of some wall-walking demon.

Every so often, Maddy's eyes would catch the quick movements of tiny, shin-high beings on the floor. They were so spindly they were difficult to see properly. Maddy walked slowly around the circle of the clearing, eyes flitting over the foliage on the floor. She spotted two of the beings when they stopped to hastily embrace each other. They had tall antennas protruding from the tops of their smooth heads which entangled as they hugged. The next time Maddy blinked, the two had parted, scampering off into the undergrowth.

Maddy stopped beside a tree and leaned her arm against it. She felt better out from Cerulean's light; it made her feel like she was onstage, sweating beneath a spotlight. From here, she had a view of a very pretty fae creature. She was sat on a fallen log, rocking a doll on her lap and humming gently. Then the doll moved and Maddy held her breath at seeing it was a real child, a human-looking one. Their hair was a bird's nest, knotted and bushy, and their expression was so vacant they looked ill. The woman's long arms were wrapped tightly around the tiny body and her eyes were closed. It should have looked maternal, but to Maddy it simply looked wrong.

She was about to go ask Cerulean to do something about the kid, when a creature stepped out in front of her. It looked like one of the same beings who were playing the music, dishevelled and wrapped in layers of furs and leather against the cold of the night.

Maddy straightened from the tree.

'Hello, little chicken,' it rasped. 'Here on your own?'

'No.'

'Ah, well.' The thing ran his eyes from Maddy's face, all

the way down to the toes of her boots and back up again. 'Forget them, pretty human. Rollick with me, drink my wine and do my bidding. Kiss my lips when noon-night falls.' When Maddy did nothing but glare, he pulled his lip into a sneer, eyes finding the string of berries around her neck. He spat on the ground. 'Protected.'

Maddy reached up and touched the necklace. 'Yeah well, you're in my realm now you bastard.'

She felt something close to powerful, watching the thing hobble off.

'That was pretty impressive,' said a voice. Maddy turned, spotting Abi standing there, hands covered in fingerless gloves, holding a can. 'You navigated that like a pro. I see you survived your visit to hell.'

Maddy folded her arms. 'It was a close call.'

Abi smiled. 'See, told you you'd need the necklace.'

Maddy rolled her eyes and plucked at the berries. 'Yeah, this necklace of yours really came in handy. You could have told me what it was bloody for.'

Abi held up her hands. 'Woah, sorry,' she said, not sounding very sorry at all, a smile still on her lips. They were shiny with either lip-gloss or drink. 'You were kind of in a rush that night.'

'Well, I'm in no rush tonight, so spill.'

Abi tipped her head back and sighed. 'Boring. Also, you should be thanking me. You have no idea the night I had without the protection of that thing.'

'What do you mean?'

Abi pointed at her. 'You stumbled upon a fae revel that night, just like this one. You, your sister and her fairy girlfriend. As soon as they saw I'd 'lost' my necklace, they were all over me.' She shrugged. 'It's cool though. My partner was with me so things didn't get too out of hand.'

Maddy looked around at the revellers. There were more of them now, like they'd crawled out of the holes in the trees, or descended from the alien sky above. Out of the lot of them, she only counted a handful that might be human.

214

'Is your partner fae?'

'They are.' At Maddy's look, she said, 'One of the good ones!'

'How do you know? How do you know who's good?'

'Well, rule of thumb: if they're unseelie, don't go there, if they're seelie, still don't go there but less emphasis. Your Cerulean's from the former in case you were wondering. But you know, I've heard they're mellowing out over there. Less, you know, *murdery.*'

Maddy snorted. 'I disagree with that.' She looked around. 'So which one's yours?'

'That one over there. With the long hair.'

Maddy followed Abi's pointing finger to a man standing beside a tree. He was tall and thin, with hair cascading all the way down to his waist, the light colour of it catching the fire and burnishing it orange. He looked like a guy cosplaying an elf. 'He's…pretty.'

Abi smiled. 'Yeah.'

'What's his name?'

'Nevar.'

As Maddy watched, Nevar kicked back a booted foot, resting it against the tree. The firelight glinted off a small dagger sheafed there. 'Do they…do their kind often mess around with humans then?'

'Not really. But I've been around them all my life. I've known Nevar for forever. Not all of them are bad, promise.'

'Just most of them.'

'Yeah, well, it only seems that way. They're just…different. All in all, it's best to avoid.'

'Please go and tell my sister that.'

Abi clicked her tongue. 'Not sure that would work. They seem pretty smitten.'

On the far side of the fire, Cerulean was twirling Elise in some fairy dance. Well, trying to. Elise was protesting and Cerulean was smothering those protests with kisses. Maddy looked away.

'But hey,' Abi said, turning back to her, 'if you wanted

215

someone to kiss at midnight later, I'm sure I could set you up with someone here.'

'No thanks. Knowing my luck I'd get with a murdery one.'

'Okay, well you're always welcome to come kiss me and Nevar.' She grinned impishly. 'We're open to stuff like that.'

Maddy couldn't help but smile back. 'Thanks but I don't kiss boys—fairies or otherwise. *Or* their girlfriends.'

Abi shrugged. 'Suit yourself.' She ran her eyes over the revel. 'Do you want me to pick out all the humans for you?'

'Thanks, but I'm good.'

Maddy walked away, coming to a stop beside a tree and sliding down it until she was crouching. Here, the fire warmed her and she had a good view of the clearing. As long as she had Elise in her sights, she felt okay.

CHAPTER 34

She wasn't sure if it was the warmth of the fire, the alcohol or the late hour that made Maddy sleepy. She had her head resting back against the tree and if she didn't look too closely at the bodies writhing around her, she could pretend she was just at any old party out in the woods.

A body thunked down beside her, making her jump and nearly drop her drink.

'Okay, so—' Abi put down her can and tucked her hair behind her ears. Maddy noticed for the first time that it was streaked with purple. 'Fairies can't lie,' she said, beginning to count on her fingers. 'which makes them a lot more trustworthy in my opinion. That necklace you have—wards them off. It's like us smearing ourselves in dog crap or something. Not harmful, you just wouldn't want to be near them. It also stops their glamour from working on you. And yes, the four-leaved clover thing is real. Lets you see through their glamour. I've sewn them into all my shoes so I have them on me whenever I'm out. Um—iron burns the crap out of them. They are massive into tradition and honour— a bit Japanese like that, I suppose.' Abi stopped and took a breath. 'So, now you know all that, you gonna chill out and enjoy the party?'

Maddy smiled thinly. 'I just can't. It's all shit.'

Abi huffed. 'Are you a Cancer? You should really give this lot a chance. Yeah they're massive shitheads but they're not affiliated to either court, most of them, so they're just here slumming it with us humans.'

'They tried to eat me.'

Abi snorted. 'Bummer. But again, that was the unseelie court, not these lot.'

Maddy shook her head. 'They all look the same from where I'm standing.'

'We've been shit to them too, you know. The Catholic church, way back when. More than shit. Nevar still has the scars.' Seeing Maddy's frown, she threw out a hand. 'Yeah, he's kinda old.'

Maddy glanced over at Cerulean, wondering how old she truly was. She looked young—thirty at most, and even that was pushing it. But what if she wasn't—what if she was triple that, quadruple that. And Elise had only been an adult for a couple of months. Maddy's lip curled. Gross.

Cerulean was talking with a giant of a woman, with straight, blood-red hair and wings that twitched as if in time with her heartbeat. Her hand was curled around a mug and Maddy saw she had an extra finger.

Elise stood beside them, looking a little lost. Her eyes roved over the party until she spotted Maddy sitting on the ground and shot her a smile.

'Just gonna see my sister,' Maddy said, standing up. Elise met her halfway.

'Hey,' Elise said. 'Enjoying yourself?'

Maddy pursed her lips. 'It's alright. Feel a bit strange though.'

'Why?'

'Well—' Maddy gestured at the party. 'There's just more of them than us.'

Elise shook her head. 'Nope. There's way more of us. Most of them are exiled, you know? Cerulean was telling me. It's kind of sad.'

'Probably a reason for that,' Maddy retorted. 'Anyway, are *you* enjoying yourself?'

'Yeah! I mean, it's crazy but—well—I'm going to have to get used to it, aren't I? Hey look, Cerulean did something

218

to my drink. Taste it.'

Cautiously, Maddy took a sip.

'What does it taste like?' Elise said.

'Um, cherries?'

'Yeah! She changed the flavour. God, I wish we could do stuff like that. Don't you?'

'Not really. Elise, do you know how old Cerulean is?'

'Well, no, why?'

'It's just, I think they age differently. Like, slower. So they might look young but they might actually be a hundred.'

'*Oookay*, so what's your point?'

'Well, don't you think you should know? You know, before you completely give yourself up to her. She might be, like, *grooming* you.'

Elise let out a surprised laugh. 'Grooming me? Grooming me for what?'

'Well, I don't know. Just go and ask her.'

Elise shook her head. 'No. I won't. I honestly don't care.'

Maddy regarded her for a moment. 'She's changed you,' she said. 'You never used to be so…'

Elise raised her eyebrows. 'So…?'

Maddy threw out a hand. 'Well, like this. Just rash and—well—like me!'

'Oh, I see. You don't like that I'm being like you. You should like yourself more, Maddy. That's kinda sad.'

Maddy tipped her head back in frustration. 'God, I wish you would just listen to me about this! I know I'm right.'

'No. You're not. I'm not doing this, I'm not fighting with you. I'm in a really good mood tonight, Maddy. Please don't ruin it.'

'Elise, I'm not trying to sabotage—'

'Yes, you are. It's what you do. It's all you ever do.'

'Oh wow, thanks. Believe it or not, I'm actually trying to look out for you.'

Elise stepped closer. 'Listen to me, Maddy—and I mean this in the kindest way possible but—*I. Don't. Need. You.*

219

Okay? We're not little anymore. It's time we started doing our own things, separately.'

'It was you who invited me to this bloody party!'

'It's just a party, Mads! Go enjoy it, please. Go dance with that blonde girl I keep seeing you with. Just chill out.'

Maddy rolled her eyes. 'Elise, stop being so bloody naïve and open your eyes. We're surrounded by fucking monsters!'

Elise sighed. 'Maddy, don't be racist.'

Maddy put her head into her hands. 'Oh my god.'

'They're people—sentient—just like us.'

'No, they're not fucking people! We're not even the same species. You're in a relationship with someone who isn't *human*. It's fucked!'

Elise shook her head. 'I'm so done with this conversation. Just go home if you're gonna be all mardy.'

'Elise, Cerulean isn't how you think she is.'

'Oh let me guess, you know her *waaaay* more than I do. She's just evil and wants to spirit me away to her fairy world and eat my soul.'

'No, but she's deceitful. She doesn't like you as much as you think she does. I know that for a fact.'

'Maddy, why do you always have to be such a bitch?' Elise asked sadly. 'You used to be on my side, always. We used to be so close.' She sighed and turned away. 'Whatever. Just leave me alone.'

'We had sex!' When she saw she had Elise's attention again, Maddy went on, 'Me and Cerulean, we had sex.'

Elise shook her head falteringly. 'No, you didn't.'

'We did.' Maddy gestured in Cerulean's direction. 'Ask her. She can't lie. Their kind can't lie.'

Elise stared at her for a moment more before starting off towards Cerulean.

'Hey, you alright?'

Abi slid up to Maddy's side, a can of lager in her hand. It smelt awful to Maddy. She kept her eyes on Elise as she stopped in front of Cerulean. Her heart thudded

220

maddeningly. She saw Elise say a few words, relieving Cerulean of her mostly drained bottle of wine. Then she walked off into the trees alone.

'Eek, she should not be drinking that,' Abi said. 'Like, seriously.'

'Why, what's it do?'

'Messes you up. Makes you…not you.'

Maddy was about to go after Elise when Cerulean started off in that direction. She found Maddy's eyes over the fire and gave her a strange look.

'What's going on between all of you?' Abi asked.

Maddy turned to her. 'You're kinda nosy, you know that?'

Abi laughed. 'Yeah, I guess. Fine.' She gave Maddy a salute. 'I'll leave you lot to it. It's nearly midnight anyway. I need to find my fairy.'

Abi wandered off, leaving Maddy alone in the clearing. A couple of weirdos were eyeing her. She glared as she stalked past them into the trees, fiddling with the necklace to make sure they could see it.

She followed the far out glow of Cerulean's light, clunky boots tripping over logs and tree roots. The sounds of the revel were ghostly here and she wondered if she'd stumbled back into her own realm.

Elise was slumped against a tree, her gaze rooted in the direction of the revel, and of Maddy, but her expression was vacant. Even from a few feet away, Maddy could see that her pupils were shot and she had a high flush in her cheeks that reminded Maddy of old tuberculosis victims.

She stepped closer, into the ring of Cerulean's light.

'Hey Elise, maybe chill out on that wine?' Elise's eyes flicked to hers but Maddy saw no recognition in them. 'Cerulean, take it off her will you.'

'She's angry, Maddy,' Cerulean said, hands clamping down on Elise's shoulders. The wine bottle dropped from her hand, thudding off a log and landing in a pillow of moss. The pink of Elise's fingertips faded from the glass. 'Maybe

221

you can tell me why?'

'Tell you why?' Elise croaked. She shrugged off Cerulean's touch. 'Maddy said you and her had sex.' Elise drew in a couple of quick breaths before whispering, 'Did you?'

Cerulean threw Maddy a quick, curious look. 'We shared our bodies, once,' she said. 'She denied me a second time.'

Elise shook her head. 'But—' Her eyes filled with tears and spilled over just as fast. She didn't seem to notice. 'You said you loved me. You promised me so many things. You said—'

'And I hold to them. For eternity, Elise. That's what I promised you.'

'Then why'—her voice trembled—'would you have *sex* with my sister?'

'Because she wanted me to. Because it pleased me to do so. Elise, love, why does this vex you so much?'

'I think she's poly, Elise. I think they all are.'

'*Fuck off Maddy!*' Elise put her face in her hands and gave a moaning sob. 'I gave up everything for you,' she breathed. 'Literally everything. Oh god, I don't want to be here anymore.' She began to murmur over and over, 'I don't want to be here anymore, I don't want to be here anymore, I don't want to be here anymore.'

'Elise, love.' Cerulean tried to remove Elise's hands. 'I gave you my name. My *name*. Moon eyes, you do understand what that means for me?'

'Don't call me that! Oh god, I want to die. Just kill me.' She took in a shuddering breath. 'Just kill me.'

Maddy stepped forward. 'Elise, chill out—'

Elise dropped her hands. She looked at Cerulean and uttered something, something that sounded like Cerulean but wasn't, and said, 'Do it. Just kill me.' Cerulean stumbled back, shaking her head. 'Do it! Just do it, Cerulean!' Reaching out, Elise took one of Cerulean's hands and put it to her neck. She was near hyperventilation, her face red and tear-tracked.

Maddy was scared. She'd never seen Elise this way, not ever. Maddy cried out when Cerulean all of a sudden slammed Elise against the tree, both hands clenched around her neck.

'Cerulean!' Maddy ran forward and pulled at Cerulean's arm but she was tensed hard as rock. 'Oh my god, get off her!'

She caught a flash of Cerulean's face—as red as Elise's now, teeth bared. 'Cerulean, fucking hell, you're going to kill her!'

Elise struggled, slapping against Cerulean's hands. Her eyes were wide, the anguish in them replaced by fear. In a moment, her face was beet red and purpling. Maddy wrenched her eyes away. She grabbed Cerulean's wrists instead, nails digging in, and pulled as hard as she could.

'Get off her, Cerulean. Get off her, you fucking—'

Cerulean was making noises, noises that didn't sound like they were coming from her, groans through bared teeth. Elise's struggles began to weaken and Maddy let out a panicked scream.

She continued pulling at Cerulean, refusing to look at her sister, refusing to see the life drain from her.

When Elise's arms finally fell slack at her sides, Maddy squeezed her eyes shut and punched at Cerulean with a might she didn't know she possessed. Cerulean's arms dropped and so did Elise's body.

Cerulean lowered herself into a squat a few paces away, staring into the distance.

Maddy hovered where she was, looking between the two of them. She took a breath, and then another, feeling a sudden semblance of calm wash over her.

'She's not dead,' she said. 'She probably just passed out or something.'

'She's dead.' Cerulean's voice was flat. 'I wouldn't have stopped otherwise.'

Maddy stared at Elise, lying at the edge of Cerulean's light, part in shadow. Her eyes weren't closed properly.

'Wake her up then. Do something. Use your—your magic. Bring her back!'

'I can't. I told her, just party tricks.'

Cerulean stood up and kneeled at Elise's side and began rearranging her limbs. Bile rose in Maddy's throat. She turned and heaved onto the grass. 'Cerulean—' She gagged a few more times, hand up to her mouth. 'She can't be dead.'

Cerulean didn't answer. She was tucking Elise's hair behind her ears, smoothing it away from her forehead. Then she slid her arms under her body and picked her up. Her eyes were blanker than blank.

Maddy stepped away, suddenly scared for herself. 'You're a psychopath,' she breathed. 'You killed her, you fucking killed my sister!'

Cerulean turned away. Maddy released a yell and struck out, fists connecting with the solid muscle of her upper arms. Cerulean only held Elise tighter. She took two more steps then pitched herself into the air.

'Bring her back!'

Maddy dropped to her knees. She pressed her face into the mulchy earth and keened into it, hands grabbing fistfuls of dead leaves. She was vaguely aware of an arm coming over her shoulders and Abi's muffled *'God'*. In the distance she heard a chorus of cheers—it must be midnight—but to Maddy, they sounded more like screams.

Cerulean's light faded, leaving them in the darkness of the forest.

CHAPTER 35

Cerulean nocked her arrow, her breath shallow and reeking of wine. The deer stepped out from behind a bush, ears twitching and eyes distrustful. Cerulean bade herself to remain still when all she wanted to do was charge the creature and snap its neck, then snap it a second time.

Her bow wobbled. Cerulean cursed, steadying her stance and forcing herself to breathe slowly. The deer cocked its head to the left. It would flee in a moment.

Earlie stepped out behind a tree. Startled, Cerulean loosed the arrow and it speared the animal's flank with a slick thud. The deer jerked, took a stumbling step forward then fell. Cerulean lowered her bow, breathing hard, and picked up her wine bottle and drank from it deeply.

Earlie gazed down at the animal, face carefully masked. She stepped around it and approached Cerulean like one would a skittish colt. She laid a hand on her shoulder.

'You killed your mortal.'

'Get away from me, Earlie,' Cerulean bit out, 'before I wring your neck too.'

Earlie sighed but removed her hand. Cerulean raised the bottle to her lips again, ignoring how her hand shook. The pity in her sister's eyes was more than she could bear.

෧ ෨

The family's mausoleum stood at the back of the grounds, in the shadow of a wild oak tree and concealed in a way that it couldn't be seen from any of the balconies or revel places. Death was a weakness that their kind forbade. Nobody in their family had succumbed to it since conquering the unseelie court and the place stood empty.

Until now.

Cerulean had axed the rosebush that had wound itself around the cracked pillars. It'd snaked its way through the door and creeped over the white walls. In the dimness, red roses bloomed like blood spills.

The far right corner was the only place that the outside light reached, and it was here that Cerulean had laid Elise to rest. The window beside her tomb was set with blue stained glass. At certain hours of the day, light would leak through and Elise would glow like moonlight.

Cerulean entered the mausoleum with the same emptiness in her heart that had beset her yesterday, and the day before that, and she would continue to until it was her turn to lay her bones down on the cold stone. She put her wine bottle down on the floor, hating how it echoed.

A spider was creeping over Elise's cheek. Cerulean brushed it away, giving a teary chuckle at the feel of her skin—she was no colder in death than she was in life. She fingered a strand of Elise's hair, stroking over her shoulder, fingers trailing across the white dress she'd clothed her in.

She committed every minute detail to memory; this would be the last time she'd visit her.

'Elise…' Her hand hovered over Elise's, yearning to tangle their fingers together once more. 'Oh, Elise. We were just beginning, moon eyes.'

The sight of her own hands, as they often did, filled her with fury. She took them off Elise, curling them into fists at her sides. How dare she touch Elise with the same instruments which killed her.

She stared at Elise's face, still and serene in death. 'Nothing can avenge your death, my love,' she whispered, voice ragged, 'but I vow to you I will seek retribution upon myself and gladly endure it until the day I am laid down beside you.' She raised her shaking, traitorous fingers and kissed them, pressing the tips to Elise's frozen lips.

As she lowered them, she felt arms come around her and caught Earlie's floral, mulchy scent. Her body stiffened with wracking rage but after a moment she lifted her hands, securing the arms tighter around her.

'Risarial,' she called, stepping out of Earlie's embrace.

Her oldest sister entered the mausoleum, walking slowly to Elise's tomb, eyes fixed on the dead girl. She raised her hands, fingers crooked and stiff, and twisted them. Briars burst from the floor in a cloud of dust and twisted together to form a wall around Elise until she couldn't be seen anymore.

Cerulean put a palm to the wall, uncaring of the thorns which dug into her calloused palms and raked her skin. She paused to make sure her voice was steady before saying,

Sleep now, my mortal girl,
these briars and thorns to never unfurl.
A bargain set and a bargain lost,
now you lie in an eternal frost.
If a one comes to disturb you now,
their death will be swift, to that I vow.

ॐ ॐ

Later that day, Cerulean packed a bag. In it was clothes, some food for her journey and nothing more. She ignored Earlie's tears; swatted her hands away as she held out framed portraits of them for her to take; pushed passed Risarial who blocked her bedroom doorway, eyes orange with disapproval.

She left home without another word. Her journey took her through orchards and along beaches, over meadowed hills and copses of birch trees. She ignored the dryads who reached down for a touch of her hair and snarled at clouds of sprites who fluttered around her, pressing their tiny mouths to any spot of bared skin.

Her father's subjects fell away and the rich, misty lands faded into the rocky, perilous terrain of the bowls of her court.

Creatures hissed at her light, throwing gnarled arms over their eyes and cowering back into the shadows. A redcap spat at her boots, touching two fingers to its cap in threat.

She entered into the vast cavern, eyes on the pool of light in the centre of it, trickling through the interwoven boughs above.

The fairy she sought was on her knees, pooling water from a vat onto the tail of a halfling. The blue-eyed creature didn't look as though she belonged on land but throw her back to sea and Cerulean was sure she'd drown.

'Litharaye.'

Litharaye looked up through limp hair the colour of charcoal, eyes glowing a touch more liquid than Risarial's did in anger.

'Heavens.' Litharaye stood slowly, gaze raking over Cerulean who stood there with naught but a satchel. Her smile was cool. She shook out her hand, running its damp palm over the short, messy hair of the halfling as she retook the seat beside her. 'To what do we owe the pleasure?'

Cerulean dropped her bag. 'I have come to swear fealty to you in order to fulfil a duty of retribution.'

Litharaye's eyebrow rose. She leaned forward, and horns, as twisted as hawthorn branches, cast shadows over her face. 'And what do you swear upon?'

'I swear upon the Dead Pantheon, the honour to my lineage, and the memory of my slain love.'

'Indeed? And who is it you seek retribution upon?'

Cerulean's throat bobbed. 'Myself. I seek it upon myself.'

Litharaye cocked her head. 'Oh. You will tell me more about this slain love of yours once you have kissed my hand.' Litharaye held out her hand, a ring set with a stone the same colour of her eyes on one finger. Cerulean grasped it and knelt. 'Cerulean, former lady of the dark court, daughter of Folred, former subject of the light court, do you swear fealty to me now and until the terms of your servitude have been worked?'

Cerulean put her lips to the amber stone. 'I swear it.'

'Do you wish to know the terms of your servitude?'

'I do not.'

Litharaye smiled, then said in a purr, 'And do you swear to pledge yourself to my subjects and our cause to bring about a new court and usurp the current throne?'

'I swear it only if my sisters' lives are spared.'

Litharaye paused, searching Cerulean's eyes. Cerulean forced herself not to blink lest the agreement be voided. 'Agreed,' Litharaye finally said. 'No harm will come to them from my hands nor those of my subjects.' She smiled cruelly. 'The same cannot be said for yours, however. Hands which have already seen much blood.' She turned Cerulean's hand over, digging her thumbnail into her palm. 'Your slain love.'

Cerulean snatched back her hand. 'Are we done?'

Litharaye inclined her head. 'For now. Rise and get out of my sight. I will call for you when I have need of you.'

CHAPTER 36

Maddy was quiet as she slipped through the backdoor of Phil's house, careful not to rattle the keys too much. There was mud on her boots as she slipped them off and she cursed quietly as it splattered over the white tiled floor.

Kicking the boots to the wall, she sniffed, using the side of one hand to wipe the tears from her cheeks. The wetness gleamed on her skin, luminous in the moonlight.

Even though it was after midnight, she still hovered at the threshold of the kitchen, listening for any signs of life. Phil's parents hated her creeping around like this—hated her staying here at all, Maddy was sure of it. Still, the pity made them obliging and Maddy would carry on being that pitiful thing for as long as she could because going back home was just not an option anymore.

After ensuring that everyone was asleep and hopefully none the wiser, she padded out of the kitchen and through the door leading to the basement. It was her room now, strewn with all the belongings she could pack into her small suitcase. Most of her clothes were still inside it since there wasn't anywhere else in the room to store anything.

At first, Phil's parents had lent her one of their spare rooms but Maddy had declined. It just felt too weird. Down here, she was less conspicuous and it was easier to leave unnoticed in the middle of the night.

She crossed over to the minifridge and pulled out a colourful can of craft beer. It had a monster printed on it, with yellow skin and purple hair, each strand as thick as snakes. Maddy rubbed her thumbnail over the monster's open mouth, wondering where the artist got their inspiration from, wondering if this monster was real.

She fell over the sagging orange sofa, kicking her feet up onto the arm. Something hard dug into her hip and she reached into her jeans pocket, pulling out the quartz crystal and glass beads in there. Feeling another wave of frustration wash over her, she tossed them away, grimacing as one of them plinked loudly off a table leg.

Earlier that night, she'd left the house with all her pockets ladened down with something—a bell from a cat's collar, a tiny jar of honey, more crystals and a small bundle of mint leaves tied with a hair bobble. All of which she'd left in the field, the one which had been choked with mist all those weeks ago. Under the moon's gaze, she waited, and waited some more, until the night's chill had forced her home again.

She didn't know if any of those offerings actually did shit but at this point, she'd try anything. Well, almost anything. A guy on the forum had posted some verbal spells too but when she'd opened her mouth to utter them, a wave of fear stopped her. There was summoning and then there was *summoning*.

Maddy sipped from her can, pissed at herself. Next time. She'd try the words next time.

Fishing her phone from her coat pocket, she navigated to that forum now. It was kind of local which was the only thing that appealed to her. It was full of whackos and Maddy had laughed dryly to herself whilst signing up. She was one of those whackos now.

She found the thread she'd started a few weeks back and posted an update of her night: *Offerings didn't work.* She hovered her thumb over her phone before pressing *submit*. There wasn't much more to say than that.

Maddy closed her eyes, beer can cooling the skin of her stomach where her top had ridden up. She was done crying but the anger still thrummed through her, hot and acidic. At this point, she wasn't even sure who it was directed at more—herself or the bastard who had strangled her sister to death and absconded with her body.

At least the police had backed off a bit now. Maddy wasn't above lying but pretending to everyone that Elise had simply disappeared following the New Year's Eve party, rather than being murdered at her own wish and then abducted into the sky by said murderer, was bit by bit killing her.

She had done her best to implicate the shit out of Cerulean. She had no hopes that the police would find her but Maddy had pledged her life to finding Elise again and any and all eyes on the case was good enough for her.

It had been no surprise at all when her parents had tried to sic the blame on her. After all, it was Maddy who had given Elise the idea of being gay in the first place and there's no way her goody-goody sister would have attended a depraved piss-up in the woods without some cajoling from her.

Maddy had let them blame her. It had made it easier to wire herself money from her mum's account and steal whatever notes and coins she could find strewn around the house. She had her passport with her too, and her birth certificate. Whatever happened, she knew she'd never go home.

When her mind drifted back to that night, to Cerulean's glittering eyes and the happy glow of her sister which faded into something horrific, to Abi, who she'd tried to find almost every night since, screaming and screaming her name in the woods until her throat was raw, she swiped away the fairy forum and opened up her dating app.

Shortly after Elise's disappearance, when the world had stopped looking at her, the thought that Cerulean was the last person she'd slept with suddenly seemed abhorrent. She'd sorted that quickly with Chloe, although the mini breakdown that had come afterwards kind of ruined the whole thing.

She found herself on the app most nights following a foiled attempt at finding her way back to Cerulean's court. She never met up with anyone, never even replied to her matches, but the thought of losing herself in another person, an innocent who didn't know any of the twisted shit that she did was strangely alluring.

Maddy put down her can and rolled onto her stomach, mindlessly swiping through the app. She'd since changed her bio; it seemed wrong having something so innocuous when everything was black inside her now. Chloe must have spotted the update as she sent Maddy a screenshot of it and a trail of question marks. Maddy ignored her and they hadn't spoken since.

Absently, she took a hold of the pendent around her neck, rubbing the milky white stone with her thumb. It was just a tic now, but each time she became aware of how cold it was, how much she yearned for it to warm, it was enough to bring her to her knees.

She put it to her lips and warmed it with her breath instead. Eyes closed, she thought of Elise. Where the *hell* was she? The thought that she was buried in some alien soil made her feel sick. And what if she'd been cremated? Who had mourned her? Not Cerulean, her murderer. Elise had no one else in that cesspit. Elise was alone and even though she was dead, Maddy knew she would hate that. Being alone had always scared Elise.

Maddy opened her eyes again but her phone screen was blurry from tears. She had never felt truly whole but this gaping wound just wouldn't stop seeping. She needed to find Elise like she needed air to breathe.

Her phone chimed. Maddy blinked, letting the tears fall. She wiped her nose and opened up the new message which popped up.

Ruth: Hey, you seem kind of fucked up. Me too x

Maddy snorted. She opened the girl's profile, wondering who the hell she'd matched with, and scrolled through her pictures. She had three. The first sported her sitting on a low brick wall, booted feet kicked out in front of her, a camera slung around her neck. Maddy nodded her approval, eyes drawn to the small tattoos on her arms. The second was a black and white selfie. She was dressed in a ribbed white tank top, of which Maddy also approved. And her hair was short—bonus points.

It was the third picture that had Maddy sitting up and gripping her phone with two hands. There was nothing all that interesting about the photo, not really, but it was one she'd seen before. On the fairy forum.

At least, she was mostly sure she had.

Minimising the dating app, she navigated back to the forum. She shook her head, wondering which thread she'd seen the photo from. She found her origin thread and scrolled quickly through the replies, stopping when a tiny thumbnail matching the photo popped up. Maddy's breath caught. They *were* the same. Holy shit, she'd found another fairy freak.

She clicked on the thumbnail, which took her to the girl's profile. All the threads she'd created and commented on were there. Maddy flicked through them quickly, a curious feeling of vindication blooming in her chest. God, this girl had been fucked over by them too—a lot, judging by all of her heated comments.

She took a screenshot of the girl's profile, switched back to the dating app and attached the screenshot to her message.

Hey, she replied. *This you?*

She tapped a nail on her phone until a reply popped up.

Ruth: Yeah. What about it?

Maddy blew out a breath, heartrate skyrocketing.

Head bowed, she quickly typed back, *We need to meet. I need your help.*

To Be Continued in

❧ GIRLS OF EARTH ❧

The next book in the Sisters of Soil series.

✦

visit **hollythornebooks.com** to join the newsletter
and keep up to date with future book news!

✦

Printed in Great Britain
by Amazon